Emily Swanson used to be a quiet, small town girl with a troubled past. Now she's a confident young woman with a bright future. But a shocking crime will threaten to end her career, if not her life.

When fellow student teacher Becky vanishes just weeks before their finals, Emily is disturbed to find no one cares. Strangely, some even seem relieved.

Soon, Emily is questioning just how well she knows her friend. Because it seems everyone has a reason to hate Becky. But what if hate has led to murder?

Suddenly caught in a deadly web of lies and pursued by those who need the sordid truth to stay buried, Emily may be Becky's only hope.

But with time running out and her own life in danger, can she find her before it's too late?

THE EMILY SWANSON SERIES #1

BAD BLOOD

MALCOLM RICHARDS

STORM
HOUSE

Available from Malcolm Richards

The Emily Swanson Series
Bad Blood
Lost Lives
Cruel Minds
Cold Hearts

The Cove Trilogy
The Cove
Desperation Point (2018)
The Devil's Gate (2018)

Standalone
The Hiding House
Walking After Midnight

Sign up for the author's New Releases mailing list.
www.malcolmrichardsauthor.com

For Ellis & Jenn

BAD BLOOD

Somerset, England
June

1

TUESDAY

THEY WERE STARING at her. She was sure of it. Staring and whispering to one another about the slight, blonde young woman sitting alone at the corner table. For twenty minutes now. Well, let them, she thought. There was nothing wrong with dining alone or enjoying a glass of wine in solitude. People did it all the time. The only problem was no one had informed her anxiety.

Emily Swanson poured herself another half glass of Pinot Grigio. *You're twenty-two, a grown woman. Not that silly little shy girl you left back home, walking with her eyes pointed at the ground.*

A waiter circled her table, glancing at the empty seats. He smiled, his expression somewhere between pity and irritation. Emily scowled until he sailed away again.

Despite the cold blast of the air conditioning, she felt her face heating up. Perhaps she should go ahead and order. They were sure to turn up soon. Or perhaps she should pay for her drink and leave. Instead, she took a sip of wine and shrank further into her seat.

Someone was calling her name. Across the restaurant, a hand flapped in her direction. Relief poured into her body, releasing the muscles. *Well, it's about time.* Smiling, she waved back at the young woman with shoulder length dark hair, who was hurrying toward her.

"Oh, my God, I'm *so* sorry. I went into campus to return the last of my library books and who should I bump into but Kerry-Anne Watkins. Christ, that girl has a mouth on her like an outboard motor! She wouldn't let me go! I'm telling you, with a case of verbal diarrhoea *that* bad she seriously needs to increase her fibre intake!" Smiling and breathless, Charlotte Walsh sat down. "Anyway, I'm here now. How are you?"

"Hungry." Emily handed her a menu and poured her a glass of wine. "Becky's not with you?"

"No, of course not. Did you honestly think she was going to come?"

"She said yesterday morning that she'd be here."

Charlotte pored over the menu. "What Becky Briar says and what Becky Briar does are rarely the same thing. Didn't I tell you the very day she moved into our humble home? I said, that girl is not interested in friendship. All she wants is a roof over her head. Why did Taylor have to move out? She was a damn slob but at least we didn't have to creep around her moods for months on end."

"But still… It's supposed to be our last dinner together. An official farewell."

"All I'm saying is don't hold your breath. Jesus, I will not miss that girl when I'm gone."

Emily stared at the empty seat next to her. "What's with all the blaspheming? If your father could hear you he'd have a heart attack."

"You noticed that? I'm getting it all out now before I go home next week. It's back to the butter-wouldn't-melt daughter of a priest's life for me. Christ on a bicycle, what am I even doing?"

"You don't have to go home, you know. There's a whole world out there."

"Says the country bumpkin." Charlotte's smile faded. "And I do have to go home. I'm all Dad's got. He would never admit it but he's been struggling since I've been away."

Emily's gaze moved to Charlotte's neck. Something was missing.

"Your necklace," she said.

Charlotte's hand reached to the space between her collarbones. "Controversial, isn't it? I figured university is over, it's the start of a new era . . . so why not start with a new me. . ."

"But it was your mother's."

"I know, but lately I've decided that my memories of her should be treasured, not worn around my neck like a stone. I've made a memory box. It'll be safe in there. It's strange, but I feel lighter without it." Charlotte's eyes had become wet and glossy. "Speaking of new eras, I can't believe you're going to be a teacher. It's amazing, Emily! Think of all those young lives you'll be helping to shape. And I'm going to be a historian!"

"What exactly does a historian do?"

"Beats me. Hang out at libraries, drinking tea and wearing cardigans?"

"There's nothing wrong with wearing cardigans."

Charlotte smiled. "Anyway, have you made a decision about Principal Talbot's offer? Or has your mother finally guilt-tripped you into returning home?"

Emily slumped in her seat. She didn't want to think

about her mother, who'd already called twice today.

"Let's order food."

"You're running out of time, you know."

"Thanks for the reminder." She stared at the menu. She hated menus. With so many things to choose from, how did you know if you were picking the right dish?

The waiter came over. "Are you expecting someone else?"

Emily's eyes drifted to the empty seat. Perhaps Becky would still show up. It would be a shame if she didn't.

Charlotte ordered first. Emily stumbled and stammered then blushing, picked a dish at random—rice and fish in some sort of marinade. When the waiter had left them, she pulled out her phone.

"Phones at the dinner table? Really?" Charlotte said with a wink.

"I'm going to call Becky. She should be here."

As Emily waited for the line to connect, her mind wandered back to yesterday morning. Becky had been sullen as usual, and half awake, but she'd agreed to come for what would be their last dinner together as housemates. Not just as housemates, Emily realised. A thought struck her: she hadn't heard Becky come home last night. She had been out most evenings lately, but Emily would always wake up to the slam of the front door late at night, and the stomp of Becky's feet on the stairs.

The phone rang for a long time before connecting to an automated voicemail service. She hung up without leaving a message.

"When did you last see Becky?"

Charlotte was busy snapping a bread stick in half. She shrugged a shoulder. "Sunday. Maybe."

"You didn't see her last night?"

"I came home around nine. You were in your room. I assumed Becky was either in hers or out. Those are the two places you can usually find her." She glanced at Emily. "Why?"

Emily shook her head.

"She's not here because she doesn't *want* to be, Em. She doesn't care. I know it's not nice to hear but it's the truth."

Staring at the empty seat, Emily heaved her shoulders. It wasn't as if Becky ever socialised with them.

"You're probably right," she said.

An uneasy feeling fluttered in her stomach.

2

WEDNESDAY

QUANTOCK UNIVERSITY WAS a small and relatively new institution. Built in the late eighties and situated thirty minutes west of Glastonbury, the university had been named after the Quantock Hills, England's first designated Area of Natural Outstanding Beauty. It was a shame, Emily had thought on her very first day, that the campus didn't reflect such a title. Apart from a few uninspired green areas, Quantock University was a maze of flat-roofed, concrete buildings devoid of personality. Fortunately, its outstanding reputation in the areas of teaching and humanities more than made up for its lack of aesthetics.

Emily walked through the university gates just after four o'clock. The campus was a swirl of chatter. Hordes of students piled in and out of lecture halls and classrooms, and filled recreation areas. Above, the sky was a clear blue with a smattering of clouds. The afternoon sun was warm and pleasant.

Becky had not returned home last night. Emily had checked her room this morning before heading off to her teaching placement at High Mount Secondary School. She had not responded to Emily's texts or to the two voicemail messages she'd left during her morning break and lunch hour. By the time the afternoon had come around, Emily was distracted and anxious, and had found it difficult to control her cohort of young students. As soon as school had ended and the children had become someone else's responsibility, she'd slipped out and headed straight to the campus.

Reaching the quad, she scanned the plethora of young men and women milling about in pairs and groups. Some shared smiles and laughter while others sat in tight circles, discussing the state of the world. Emily's gaze moved from group to group. Becky was not among them.

Moving on, she headed for the Sullivan building, home to the teaching and education department, and where she had spent much of the first three years of her degree. A long hall ran the length of the building, with rooms on both sides. A group of students whom Emily knew from class strolled by. None of them had seen Becky for a long time. Two of them thought she had quit university. None seemed particularly concerned by her disappearance.

Emily continued down the hall, peering into empty rooms. Lectures were almost finished for the year. Soon, the campus would become a ghost town.

One lecture room had a single occupant. Emily knocked on the door. A calm voice ushered her in. Bill Creed sat behind his desk, busy marking test papers.

"Miss Swanson," he said, his face lighting up with a brilliant smile. "To what do I owe the pleasure?"

Bill was in his early thirties, younger than most of the lecturers in the education department. He was handsome in a boyish kind of way, his green eyes and long, dark lashes a talking point among some of his more enamoured students.

And, unlike most of the other lecturers in the education department, he wore no wedding ring, sparking fierce debate over his relationship status and sexual orientation.

"Hello, Bill," Emily said, offering him a subdued smile. "I'm looking for Becky Briar. I don't suppose you've seen her?"

Bill leaned back in his chair and interlinked his fingers across his chest. "Ah, the ever-elusive Miss Briar. As much as I would love to say I've seen her, you and I both know we'd have a greater chance of seeing a bear in a nun's outfit wandering the halls of the Sullivan building." He paused to scribble notes on a student paper. "Have you tried the bar?"

"It's a little early in the day, isn't it?" Emily glared at him, offended on Becky's behalf.

Leaning forward, Bill flashed his green eyes. "I'm sorry. That was a little harsh. It just frustrates me that after almost four years of teaching and learning and toiling away, that Becky would wait until it's almost all over to go and screw it up. She had the makings of a good teacher. Now I doubt she'll be allowed to take the exams. What *is* going on with her?"

Emily shoulders slumped. "I don't know. She's been so distant lately. She's either out all the time or hiding in her room. She's always in a bad mood and she just won't talk about it. I'm worried."

"I hear you. I've tried on numerous occasions to reach her, but she has yet to return a single phone call."

Emily looked up.

"Let's just say I had to do some damage control after she stopped attending her teaching placement," Bill said.

Emily tried to hide her shock by staring at the floor. She'd had no idea that Becky hadn't been attending her placement. Missing lectures was one thing, but without the placement, her chances of qualifying as a teacher were zero.

Mistaking her expression for cynicism, Bill said, "Believe it or not, Emily, some of us lecturers actually care about our students. Some of us even want our students to do well — and not just because your results reflect our teaching skills."

And pay grade, Emily thought. She stared across the lecture hall, at the rows of empty chairs. "Well, I don't know what's going on with Becky."

She thought about sharing her concerns over Becky's whereabouts but decided against it. There was the possibility that she'd stayed over at a friend's, or a boy's, and that she was back home right now, sleeping off a hangover. So why was there a knot of anxiety growing in Emily's stomach?

"I'll say it again—it's a real disappointment she's not going to make it through the exams. It's a waste of everyone's time and effort. Including Miss Briar's." Bill swept his hair away from his eyes and flashed Emily a smile. "But thank goodness for the likes of you. I've heard nothing but good things from Principal Talbot. He tells me he's offered you a post at High Mount. They'll be very lucky to have you."

Blushing, Emily dug her hands into her pockets. "I haven't accepted it yet."

"Oh? Why not?"

Emily shrugged a shoulder.

"Well, I'll be here, pen poised, ready to write you a glowing reference when you do."

She thanked him, noting with discomfort how his gaze lingered a little too long.

"Well, if you see Becky, would you ask her to call me?"

Leaving the Sullivan building, Emily headed to the cafeteria. Groups of students sat at tables picking at sandwiches and cold pizza slices. Next, she stopped by the Students' Union building, which housed the student welfare centre and, just along from it, the student bar. Emily had always found that amusing: pour out your sorrows then drown them in tequila shots. There were already a few young patrons huddled around tables in the dimly lit bar, and a couple of women bent over the pool table, their eyes narrowed with concentration.

The last place Emily could think of to check was the theatre. She'd heard Becky mention her 'actor friends' a few times in the past. Most students tended to stick to their own tribes. Emily had seen it countless times in the cafeteria: English literature students on one table, psychology on another, the artists all gathered in the quad, smoking roll ups. Becky was different. It was as if she'd chosen the wrong path and had regretted it ever since.

"Teachers suck," she'd once said, on a rare occasion she had sat next to Emily during a lecture. Emily had wondered if Becky had been referring to her.

The theatre was small and modern with black walls and laminate flooring; the stage unremarkable but purposefully so, Emily thought. A blank page on which to create. No one was around but she could hear voices floating out from backstage. A sign on a door to the right of the stage read: GREEN ROOM.

Emily hesitated. Actors and performers always seemed to hold themselves in high regard. For a moment, she wondered what they would think of her; a quiet country girl, who had worked hard to lose most of her accent, and had no creative leanings whatsoever. That wasn't entirely true. She loved to garden, and if planting seeds and nurturing them until they bloomed with life couldn't be called creative, well, she didn't know what could.

Shrugging off her nerves, she entered the green room. Students dressed in loose clothing, most of whom were ridiculously good looking, milled about. Some were busy rehearsing lines in a corner. Others lounged on beanbags, idly chatting while staring at phone screens. All of them looked up as Emily came closer. Some regarded her unfamiliar face with curiosity. Most returned to their conversations, uninterested in this pretty but forgettable young woman who had entered their domain.

Emily searched the room with her eyes. Becky was not here. A handsome young man, tall and lithe, broke away from a group and bounded up to Emily.

"Hi," he said, his deep brown eyes, earnest and soulful. "You look a little lost."

Emily told him she was looking for her friend, that she knew she sometimes hung out here.

"Oh, Becky, sure. Yeah, she's here sometimes. I think she has a not-so-secret desire to tread the boards. God knows why she's training to be a teacher. What's that saying? *Those who can't do, teach.*"

Emily smiled through tight lips. "Has she been around the last couple of days?"

"I'm not sure. Just a minute." The young man turned and addressed the other actors.

"She was supposed to meet a group of us at the bar on Monday night," another equally handsome young man said, "but she called to cancel."

"Did she say why?"

"Just that she had to be someplace else." The young man

shot a glance at his friends. "Is there something wrong?"

Mild concern rippled through the group. Emily shook her head. She didn't even know *if* Becky was missing yet. "If you see her, can you tell her to call me?"

Leaving the theatre, Emily did one more sweep of the campus before making her way to the bus stop. She tried Becky's number again. This time, it went straight to voicemail without ringing.

The bus appeared at the corner and began its approach. Emily considered what she should do now. Did she call the police and file a missing persons report? Did she call Becky's parents? The bus pulled in and she boarded. She would go home first. That was what she would do. And when she found Becky slouched on the sofa or playing her music too loudly in her room, she would give her a piece of her mind for making her worry.

The bus pulled away from the kerb. Emily stared out of the window, the anxious knot in her stomach growing into a ball.

3

EMILY'S HOME WAS situated on the outskirts of town. Her first year of university had been spent living on campus in student accommodation. The constant noise and partying had been manageable at first. She had even spent a few memorable evenings in various rooms, drinking her first drinks and making friends—including Charlotte Walsh. But once the settling in period was over and it was time for serious study, living on campus became intolerable.

She'd found herself making the three-hour journey back to Cornwall at weekends, just so that she could work in peace. This appeased her mother, who had been having difficulty adjusting to living alone, but being away from her friends at weekends left Emily feeling lonely.

When Charlotte suggested finding a house together, Emily agreed without a moment's thought. After a long search, they found a large three-bedroom house on the outskirts of town. There were several repairs needed, and the décor had been untouched since the seventies (green paisley print wallpaper, swirly red carpets), but the rent was cheap and the street was quiet.

Emily and Charlotte had lived there for the past three years. Taylor had lived with them for the first two. Then she'd fallen pregnant and had decided to keep the baby. Emily had put up a Room to Rent notice in the education building, and Becky had responded. She hadn't been their ideal choice, but it was an awkward time of year to find the perfect housemate, and neither of them had the money to cover the rest of the rent.

Now, Emily and Charlotte stood in the centre of Becky's bedroom, surrounded by a sea of clothes, and inhaling days old air.

"I think you're overreacting. This isn't the first time that Becky's gone AWOL," Charlotte said, wrinkling her nose in disgust.

Emily folded her arms across her chest and gazed at the debris. "I don't know. It feels different this time. No one's seen her. No one knows where she is. I've sent her texts and left voicemails... I don't think she would leave us worrying like this."

"Then you don't know Becky as well as you think you do."

"She's obviously been going through something lately. We've both been on the receiving end of her mood swings. She's missed too many lectures, failed assignments. . . Bill told me she hasn't been turning up to her teaching placement." Emily paused, deep lines forming across her brow. She moved over to the dresser where a battered old jewellery box sat on top, along with a mess of plastic beads and an array of makeup. "Whatever's been going on with Becky, perhaps it's connected to why she's disappeared."

"Or perhaps you're jumping to conclusions." Charlotte shuddered at the sight of a cereal bowl on the bedside cabinet, its contents left to fester.

"I'm going to phone around. If no one else has seen her

then I think it's time to contact her parents."

"Fine."

Emily gave the room another sweep with her eyes as Charlotte headed for the door.

"She'll probably come walking in any minute, you know."

"I hope you're right. I really do."

But Charlotte wasn't right. Emily returned to her bedroom, relieved to be surrounded by neatness and order once again, and began making phone calls. Twenty minutes later, Becky's whereabouts were still a mystery, and all Emily had managed to do was spread her anxiety to others. Even Charlotte had taken to checking her phone and coming in and out of Emily's room. A little past 9 PM, Emily placed a call to Becky's parents.

Mrs Briar answered. She and her husband hadn't heard from Becky in days.

"That's nothing new, mind you," she said, but the worry in her voice was unmistakable. "I'll try calling her. Perhaps she's just blowing off steam before the finals. I know she's been working so hard lately. I was young and a student once. I remember how stressful those last months can be."

Emily opened her mouth then closed it again. She did not want to be the one to inform Mrs Briar her daughter had been telling lies.

"I'll call her," she said again. "I'm sure it's nothing to worry about."

By then her voice had become high and tremulous.

Emily had hoped to feel reassured by Mrs Briar's words. Instead, her anxiety clambered into her chest.

All she could do now was sit and wait. Perhaps try and study for a while. She tried for twenty minutes, until a rumble in her stomach reminded her she hadn't eaten since the morning.

She was about to head down to the kitchen when her phone rang. But it was not Mrs Briar calling. It was Emily's friend, Angela Jackson.

"Sorry, I only just listened to your message. I was studying," she said, high-pitched and breathless. "Has Becky turned up yet?"

"No. I just talked to her mum. No one's seen her."

There was a brief pause before Angela spoke again. "I saw her. I saw Becky."

"What? When?"

"Monday evening at uni. She was with a guy. They were having a fight." She paused again. "Emily, she got into the car with him and he drove off."

Emily's heart began to thump in her chest.

"What guy?" she said.

4

THE CAMPUS BY evening was a very different place. Studiousness had vanished, replaced by an atmosphere of excitement and frivolity. Hordes of young people swarmed around the entrance of the Students' Union building. It didn't matter that it was Wednesday, or that for some there were classes to attend come the morning. For Emily and her peers, these were the final weeks of student life before being thrown precariously into the adult world. They had to be celebrated.

Emily strode past the building and its loud music, heading for the quad. Angela was sitting at one of the picnic tables, poring over a heavy looking textbook. The sun was setting, casting the quad in tangerine light and making Angela's frizzy red hair shimmer like fire. She was a tall and thin young woman, with a milky complexion and large, thick-rimmed glasses, and she wore a shirt with green and white stripes buttoned all the way to the top.

As Emily approached, Angela waved a hand then closed her book.

Like Emily, she was quiet and studious. The two had been friends since the day Angela had sat next to Emily in their first lecture. Although she was gangly and awkward, dropping her pen three times while scribbling down notes and constantly pushing her glasses back up her nose, Emily recognised a stillness in her that was comfortably familiar. But where living away from home had bestowed Emily with a quiet confidence, Angela had remained endearingly nervy. Emily liked her a lot.

Emily went to take a seat but Angela nodded to the left, where a couple sat entwined in each other's arms, indulging in some heavy petting.

"Library," she whispered. Gathering up her books, she scurried off.

Emily caught up with her at the library doors and they went in together. Immediately, they were immersed in a comforting hush. Moving past the librarian's desk, they headed for the study bay. The librarian, a conservatively dressed man in his early sixties, smiled and tapped his wristwatch.

"I'm closing in twenty minutes, girls," he said in a hoarse whisper.

Ignoring the fact that he'd addressed them as *girls*—she hadn't worn her hair in pigtails in quite some time—Emily nodded and said, "We only need ten."

Finding a private nook, Emily and Angela sat down. They stared at each other for a tense second.

"Tell me what you saw," Emily said.

Angela heaved her shoulders. A deep frown burrowed into her brow.

"It was the end of the day," she began. "I'd stopped by to drop off some library books. I was crossing the car park, heading back to Bessie, when I heard raised voices. I saw Becky with this guy. They were arguing. It looked heated. Lots of finger-pointing and hands in the air. Neither of them seemed to care how much noise they were making."

"Who was the guy? Did you recognise him?"

"I don't know his name, but I've seen him around. He's tall and he's built. A white guy, with cropped hair, about our age."

It didn't sound like any man Emily had ever seen Becky with, but as she was quickly learning, that didn't mean much. "He's a student?"

Angela nodded. "I think so. I've seen him at the bar a couple of times—not that I go in there much."

"What were they fighting about?"

"I wasn't close enough to hear, but whatever it was, they both looked like they wanted to tear each other apart. For a second, I thought it was going to turn violent. I had my phone out, ready to call security. But then it went quiet. They both got into his car. It was a black convertible BMW. He started the engine and they drove away."

Emily did not like what she was hearing. "Do you remember the time?"

Angela thought about it, her large eyes moving from side to side. "Class had just finished so… I guess it must have been around six. She didn't come home?"

"No. She didn't."

They were both quiet for a minute. Who was this man with the black car? There were over two thousand students at the university and whole swathes that Emily could readily admit to having never seen before.

"We need to find out who he is," she said.

Angela swallowed and ran a hand through her hair. "I think that's a bad idea. Whoever he is, he looks the type who wouldn't think twice about hitting a woman."

"Even more reason to find out if Becky's with him now."

She pulled out her phone, prompting Angela to point at a poster on the wall that said: STRICTLY NO MOBILE PHONES.

"Just keep a look out, will you?"

Emily tapped the screen and opened the Facebook app. Finding Becky's profile, she began to sweep through her pictures.

Angela looked from side to side, occasionally pushing her glasses up the bridge of her nose as she kept watch for the librarian.

There weren't many photographs to search, and even fewer taken recently. The man Angela had described was not among them. Next, Emily checked to see if Becky had left any recent updates. The last one she'd written had been back in May. It succinctly said: FUCK THIS.

Emily stood, prompting Angela to do the same.

"What now?" she said. "Because I have to get home and mentally prepare for tomorrow. There's this boy in my class—Daniel Ballinger—Anyone would think he was the teacher and I was the student."

Emily said nothing as they made their way to the exit, smiling politely at the librarian. Once they were through the doors and back in the quad, Emily said, "You've seen this guy in the bar?"

"Yes, but-"

Grabbing Angela by the arm, Emily headed for the Students' Union building. Inside, they walked the long corridor to the bar, skirting past students in various degrees of inebriation. Dance music boomed. Conversations weaved together to form a tremendous roar.

Negotiating the heaving crowds and surging bodies, Emily wound her way into the room. Standing on tiptoes, she strained to see over the heads and shoulders of her fellow students. Young men and women stood shoulder to shoulder, heaving and jostling. Beer splashed. Colourful lights dazzled and flashed. The bass thundering from the speakers made Emily's bones rattle.

"Do you see him?" she yelled.

Angela whipped her head from side to side, wincing and flinching as a group of muscle-bound sports students almost mowed her down as they pushed their way into the crowd.

She shouted something but her voice was lost in the din.

Above the bar, the LED screen began to flash, announcing a two-for-one deal on tequila shots for the next thirty minutes. Immediately, the hordes stampeded toward the waiting bar staff.

There was no way they were going to find the man in here.

Retreating, they moved back along the corridor and exited the building. Angela's shoulders, which were almost touching her ears, relaxed a little.

"I need to go home," she said.

Emily was feeling increasingly troubled. Becky had been missing for two days now. She'd last been seen disappearing in a car with a dangerous looking man who had fought bitterly with her. And before that, she'd been set on a self-destructive path that Emily and Charlotte, and everyone else for that matter, had been too preoccupied to do anything about.

"Emily, I really need to-"

"Sure. You should go. Thanks for your help."

Angela didn't leave. She hovered next to Emily, shifting from one foot to the other.

"What are you going to do now?" she asked. "I mean, about Becky?"

Emily had already made up her mind. "I'm going to call Mrs Briar again. I think it's about time the police were involved."

5

MRS BRIAR HAD reacted to Emily's findings as expected. Once she had calmed enough to speak, she'd told Emily she would file a missing persons report with the police right away, and that she would call back with an update.

It was dark when Emily returned home. The only light on was at the back of the house, in the mauve painted kitchen, where she found Charlotte snacking on rye bread and peanut butter.

"Have you heard anything?" Charlotte asked.

When Emily told her what she'd learned, she took one look at the bread and dumped it on the plate.

"What kind of car did you say?"

"A black convertible BMW. Do you know it?"

"Maybe. From the description that sounds like…I mean, I can't be sure but-"

The doorbell rang. At the same time, Emily's phone began to buzz. The women stared at each other. Charlotte went for the door. Emily pressed her phone to her ear.

"It's Heather Briar, Becky's mum." Her voice was strained, her words unsure of themselves. "The police have to make a risk assessment. They're sending an officer over to ask you some questions."

Emily heard the crackle of the police radio before

Charlotte returned.

"They've just arrived."

"You must tell them everything you know," Mrs Briar insisted. "Everything."

Emily promised that she would.

Initial Investigating Officer Andrews was very tall and slim, and looked far too young to be protecting the nation's citizens. His job, he told them as they sat in the dimly lit living room, was to reassess the risk level of Becky's disappearance that had been made based on Mrs Briar's phone call and, with permission, to search Becky's room.

He began by asking questions: When had they last seen Becky and where? What kind of mood had she been in? Had Becky displayed any unusual behaviour lately? Did she have a history of mental illness? Any addiction issues or struggles with debt?

Emily and Charlotte answered as best they could: They'd last seen her at home at the weekend, and she'd been in a bad mood or hungover, or both; the last few months, she'd been increasingly shut off from them; she'd all but given up on her studies; and yes, sometimes she'd be gone for a day, sometimes two, but she always checked in by replying to Emily's concerned texts. There was no history of mental health that they knew of, but there was a chance she was depressed. Also, no obvious debt issues judging by the fact that Becky was out most nights.

This steered the interview toward Monday evening and the fight Angela had witnessed.

Officer Andrews looked up from his notepad. "Did Miss Jackson recognise the man Becky was fighting with?"

"No. Just that he was stocky with cropped hair, and that he was behaving aggressively."

"What about the make of the car?"

"A black BMW, a convertible." Emily turned to Charlotte. "Before Officer Andrews came, you seemed like you recognised it."

Charlotte squirmed beside her. She shook her head. "Well, it sounds like you're talking about Damien Harris. But why on earth would Becky be hanging around with him?"

"Who's Damien Harris?" Officer Andrews asked.

Crossing and uncrossing her arms, Charlotte avoided his gaze. "I don't want to get anyone in trouble…"

"But. . . ?" Emily said.

"Well, from what I hear he sells drugs around campus. Mostly recreational stuff—weed, pills — that sort of thing." Her face glowed as she stared at the lurid red carpet. "That's the rumour, anyway."

"What else do you know about Damien Harris?" Officer Andrews asked.

"I think he's a chemistry student. Which figures."

"Would Mr Harris and Miss Briar have a romantic connection?"

Charlotte glanced at Emily, who shrugged a shoulder. "I don't know. Becky was involved with different guys at different times. Nothing serious, though. And from what I hear, Damien seems to change girlfriends every couple of weeks or so."

"I see."

"There's something else," Charlotte said. "Last year, Damien put another student in hospital after beating him unconscious with his bare hands. Michael Nowak or something." She turned to Emily. "You know him?"

Emily shook her head.

"I'm not sure what started it but apparently, Michael was a mess. I'm talking broken bones. You never heard about that, Em?"

Emily shrugged. "He didn't get kicked out?"

"You'd think so, wouldn't you? But somehow, he managed to get away with it. No charges were brought against him, so the rumour mill goes."

Officer Andrews frowned as he filled his notepad. "Anything else that stands out from the last few weeks?"

Both Emily and Charlotte shook their heads.

Leading Officer Andrews upstairs, Emily stood in the doorway as he conducted a search of Becky's room. Her suitcases were still under the bed. Her mostly black clothes still hung in the wardrobe. Emily didn't know if any were missing.

"What about Becky's family?" Officer Andrews sifted through the various trinkets on top of the dresser. "Any trouble there?"

"Becky never really spoke about her family."

"What about when they came to visit?"

"They never did."

Officer Andrews looked up.

"It's true." Emily didn't want to mention that her mother had also never visited during the last four years.

Officer Andrew flipped open a jewellery box. A tiny ballerina leapt up. Tinkling music began to play a familiar lullaby. The ballerina began to slowly spin around, frozen in a pirouette. The police officer searched the box's contents and plucked out a roll of papers.

"Looks like receipts for a pawn shop," he said. "Becky must have been having financial problems after all."

Emily moved up and glanced over his shoulder.

"Well, I can't see anything else out of the ordinary in here," Officer Andrews said, dropping the receipts back inside the jewellery box and closing the lid.

"What happens now?"

"I should probably speak to your friend Angela, and I think a chat with Mr Harris is in order, don't you?"

Emily led him back downstairs where Charlotte was waiting in the hallway.

"I know it's difficult but try not to worry," the police officer continued. "It seems like Becky is having problems with her studies, perhaps with drugs. There's a chance she's gone off somewhere to lie low for a while and she'll return soon."

"What if she doesn't?" Emily asked.

Officer Andrews gave her a reassuring smile. "Talk to your friends. Use social media. Ask around campus again. Someone may know something who's yet to come forward. In the meantime, once I've made my enquiries, I'll need to report back to my supervisor, and we'll go from there."

"What does that mean?" Emily said. It sounded a lot like: *if we decide there's a risk we'll investigate further.*

Officer Andrews offered her a reassuring smile. "Will it help if I tell you nearly all people reported missing are found unharmed within forty-eight hours?"

"I suppose."

But it didn't help. The feeling of dread that had been manifesting since Becky's disappearance remained after Officer Andrews had left, and she and Charlotte had returned to the living room.

They sat in silence for a long time, occasionally shooting nervous glances at each other.

"What now?" Charlotte asked.

"We do what Officer Andrews says. We keep asking questions." Emily drummed her fingers against her knees. "And we hope Becky comes home soon."

6

THURSDAY

THE MORNING PASSED slowly, as if time was wading through molasses. Emily stood at the front of the classroom with one eye on the clock as she attempted to discuss the moral compass of William Golding's Lord of the Flies. Her students had sensed her mounting agitation and were reacting as young teenagers do. It was only when she threatened them with lunchtime detention that they settled into quiet study. She was thankful for it too because when the lunch hour eventually arrived, she needed every minute.

Now alone in class and sat in front of her laptop, she set about implementing her plan of action. First, she posted a round of shout-outs on Facebook and Twitter, asking for information about Becky's whereabouts, and asking people to share the news that she had been reported missing. Next, she went through her address book and called up friends to ask what they knew about Damien Harris. Those who were aware of him were either unable or unwilling to talk. His reputation, it seemed, was intimidating enough to instil caution. She did, however, glean a couple of interesting facts. The first, that he did indeed have a current girlfriend.

And the second, that it wasn't Becky Briar.

Her name was Tamara and she was a first year Business Studies student who, according to Emily's source, was every bit as scary as Damien Harris. Once Emily had discovered her identity, she called the police station and asked to speak to Officer Andrews. The desk sergeant told her that he was out on a call and unlikely to return to the station until late that afternoon.

"I have very important information regarding the disappearance of Becky Briar," Emily said. "Please ask him to call me as soon as he can."

The desk sergeant sounded mildly amused as he jotted down her message.

The afternoon passed at a similar, sluggish pace as the morning. Emily grew increasingly anxious. It didn't help that her lunch remained uneaten in her locker. As soon as the final bell rang out, she ushered her students out of the classroom and into the playground, then hurried to the staffroom to grab her belongings. As she raced along the corridor, she saw Principal Talbot coming out of his office. Ducking into an empty classroom, she waited until he had passed by before taking off again toward the exit. She had still not made a decision about his job offer and right now, there were more pressing matters to attend to.

A heavy rain shower was in full swing as Emily entered the campus just after 4 PM. Pulling her jacket collar around her neck, she hurried to the library. Angela was waiting inside, her wet hair hanging about her shoulders like rags. She nervously told Emily about her interview with Officer Andrews, while Emily shared the information Charlotte had revealed about Damien Harris.

"What will happen now?" Angela swept her hair behind her back.

"Officer Andrews is trying to locate Damien. He says he'll know more once they've spoken."

"What was Becky doing hanging around with a drug dealer?"

"At a guess, buying drugs?"

Angela blushed. She removed her glasses and began mopping up rain from the lenses with the sleeve of her cardigan. "I shouldn't be surprised that he's a criminal, really. How else can he afford that car? Do you really think they were fighting over drugs?"

It was a question Emily had asked herself several times last night when she should have been sleeping. Officer Andrews had found no evidence in Becky's room to suggest a drug habit, and in the time Becky had lived in the house, Emily had seen nothing either. That didn't mean much, though. Emily was beginning to realise that Becky Briar's life was one big secret.

Her lenses dry, Angela popped her glasses back on her nose. "Anyway, why am I here? I've got reports waiting to be written at home, and after being interviewed by the police last night, my nerves can't take any more trouble."

"Don't worry," Emily said, standing. "You're just here to keep me company. You won't need to do any of the talking."

Grabbing her bag, Angela hurried after Emily. "Talking to who?"

"Officer Andrews said I should keep asking questions, so that's what I'm going to do."

Outside, it had stopped raining and the sun was breaking through the clouds. Emily made her way to the Business and Economics block, with Angela close behind.

"Ask questions to who? Emily, where are we going?"

Emily held the door open for Angela.

"We're going to see Damien's girlfriend," she said.

Angela's eyes grew wide with alarm. She opened her mouth to protest. Then, expelling a deep sigh, she pushed her glasses back up her nose, and followed behind.

The drone of an electric bell announced the end of class. The lecture hall doors swung open and bodies swarmed out. Nothing had changed since school: it didn't matter how engaging the lecture, as soon as the bell rang real life resumed.

Emily and Angela pressed themselves up against the wall as students filed out. Once she'd learned Tamara's name, it had been easy to track down her Facebook profile and discover what she looked like. She was petite, white, blonde-haired and blue-eyed, with a penchant for heavy makeup and expensive looking jewellery. The type of person, Emily observed, whose parents paid for university, and who had no worries about where her next meal was coming from.

It didn't take long to spot her. She was heading a group of four young women whose attire seemed better suited for evening wear rather than a lecture on free market economics. They drifted toward the exit, mobile phones already in hands, leaving behind a heady cloud of perfume as potent as tear gas.

Emily glanced at Angela, who was pressed up against the wall, her drying hair now beginning to puff and frizz.

"Come on."

"Emily, I don't. . ." Angela began, but Emily was already

ploughing ahead, determined not to lose her target in the crowd.

She followed them out through the doors and into the quad, where all four pulled out packs of menthol cigarettes and lit up. The benches were still wet from the rain, so they huddled together in a half circle, chatting among themselves and shooting disapproving glares at passers-by.

Emily hovered at the edges of the quad, a tight, anxious feeling blossoming in her chest. She was back at school, too scared to talk to the popular girls in case they mocked her.

Beside her, Angela had dug her hands so deep inside her trouser pockets they were threatening to tear right through.

"I really think we should go now." Her gaze flicked toward Tamara and friends. "I've got a hundred and one things to do, plus I have to study for the finals."

"You're not going anywhere," Emily breathed. "You're my backup if things turn ugly."

Angela's complexion grew paler.

Taking a deep breath, Emily pushed herself off the wall. Drawing closer to the group, she heard snippets of conversation.

"I'm totally freaking out—we have two weeks to the exams and I haven't studied a damn thing."

"Me either!"

"Everyone knows the first year doesn't count for shit, so chill out. You're giving me a headache."

Emily mentally shook her head. First years, she thought. They had no idea.

The group continued to talk, barely aware that Emily was standing in front of them. Again, that old school feeling returned to her—the feeling of being invisible.

At last, one of the girls looked up. She nudged Tamara,

who barked at her not to interrupt while she was texting.

Emily cleared her throat. At first, words wouldn't come.

"Hi," she said at last. She paused, giving the friends enough time to share curious side glances. "Are you Tamara?"

Tamara stared right back, her deep blue eyes turning as cold as the Arctic.

"Who wants to know?"

Emily glanced away for a second, spying Angela still pressed up against the wall as if she were waiting for a firing squad.

"I'm Emily Swanson. I was hoping you could help me with something. A friend of mine has gone missing. Becky Briar? I was wondering if you'd seen her."

Tamara glared. Her friends did the same. "Never heard of her."

Undeterred, Emily pulled out her phone and flicked through the on-screen folders. "I have a picture I can show you. Maybe you'd recognise her. She's a final year Education student. She's been missing since Monday."

Emily found the photograph she was looking for—an image snapped eight months ago on a rare night out, back when Becky was still attending classes and was less hostile. Emily stood in the centre of the picture, an awkward smile on her lips, while her housemates stood either side.

Tamara stared at the picture, her lips pulled tight and her eyes narrow.

"Do you recognise her?" Emily pressed.

"Should I?"

"Well, it's just that-"

A dark veil of anger fell across the young woman's face. "I've never seen that girl. I don't know anything about her, and I don't know why you're coming over here, singling me out, like you think I have something to do with it."

"To do with what, exactly?"

The look on Tamara's face made Emily take an involuntary step back. "I'm asking because Becky is a friend of Damien's. I assumed you might know her too."

Emily watched the seed she had planted quickly take root.

"Damien?" Tamara's face twisted with anger. "She doesn't know Damien. If she did, I'd know all about it, and I'm telling you—I've never seen her fucking ugly face before!"

"She was seen arguing with him," Emily persisted, her voice barely audible over the din of lunchtime chatter.

"Seen by who?"

"They were fighting. They got into Damien's car and they drove away. Together."

Tamara's nostrils flared as she stared at the picture of Becky. She thrust a finger in Emily's direction. "I don't know who you've been talking to but they're full of shit. I don't know who this bitch is and neither does Damien. So why don't you take your cheap, ugly phone and fuck off?"

Feeling the force of Tamara's anger, Emily caught her breath. From the corner of her eye, she saw that Angela had moved up and was now positioned within earshot of the conversation. But Tamara had already redirected her attention to her phone and was furiously tapping out a text message. Her friends continued to glare. The conversation was over.

"Thanks for your time," Emily said. "I'm sure the police will have their own questions for Damien when they catch up with him."

Tamara's head snapped up. She was silent for a moment, gazing intently at Emily. "The police?"

"They're looking for him now. They want to know all about his fight with Becky and where he took her. They're . . . concerned." Emily turned on her heels. "Bye, then."

Catching Angela's eye, she headed for the cafeteria doors. She could still hear Tamara calling after her as she headed inside.

Emily sat down at the nearest empty table and waited for Angela. She appeared moments later, pushing her glasses up to the bridge of her nose.

"Well, she seemed nice," she said, flashing a worried look at the door.

"She's lying. She recognised Becky's picture, I'm sure of it. She *knows* something."

"That her boyfriend's a lying scoundrel, probably."

Emily turned and scanned the cafeteria. She'd been holding onto a small hope that Tamara would know Becky's whereabouts, or at the very least, point her in the right direction. Yet, here she was, once again trying not to think about the terrible things that could have happened to her housemate. Pulling out her phone, she called Becky's number and was greeted by the same automated voicemail.

Who was Becky Briar? Emily had thought she'd known. Now, a veil of mystery hung over her. Lots of students experimented with drugs. It was a rite of passage for some. Emily had always been too afraid to try. But Becky…had she really developed a habit without Emily or Charlotte noticing?

Angela's voice brought Emily back to the cafeteria.

"She'll tell Damien, you know. I bet she's calling him right now." She began to drum her fingers against the tabletop. "You don't think they'll find out it was me who saw the fight? You didn't mention me, did you? Oh God, what if the police tell him it was me?"

She looked afraid now, as if she'd made a terrible mistake.

Emily shook her head. "Don't worry."

Angela was right, though. Tamara was probably warning Damien right now.

The colour had all but drained from Angela's complexion. "Will you walk me to my car?"

They walked through the building. Angela chatted nervously and glanced over her shoulder every five seconds. Emily was quiet, wondering what she should do next. She could go home and see if Becky had returned. If there was still no sign, she could call Mrs Briar to see if there had been an update from the police.

Or I could find Damien.

Panic fluttered in her stomach. It was a stupid and dangerous idea. An idea best left in the capable hands of the police.

As they entered the car park and headed toward Bessie—Angela's VW Beetle—Emily scanned the other vehicles.

"Is it here? Damien's BMW?"

Angela slid the key into the lock and opened the driver door. "I don't know. Do you need a ride home?"

Emily stood still, her eyes roaming each row of cars. How easy would it be to find Damien? She knew he was a chemistry student and she knew what kind of car he drove. That would be enough information to lead her in the right direction. Again, she felt a flutter of panic, her very cells resisting the idea.

Beside her, Angela let out a frustrated sigh. "Well, do you need a ride or not?"

Emily checked her phone. Officer Andrews still had not called. She wondered if she should try him again.

"Emily? Are you even listening to me?"

"Sorry. I think I'll walk."

"Well, I'll see you." Angela hunched her shoulders. "Please don't do anything stupid."

"Like what?"

Emily watched Angela drive away then walked back through the campus. Her mind wandered back to Damien Harris. She called the police station again to find Officer Andrews was still unavailable. This time, she was sure the desk sergeant had smirked.

Hanging up, Emily stomped through the main gates.

Why wasn't anyone taking Becky's disappearance seriously?

Because they've already made up their minds, she thought. Becky Briar was not a vulnerable child snatched from the park. She was a university drop out who was disliked by her peers, who hung around with a known drug dealer, and who had very probably been nurturing a drug habit. Becky Briar's disappearance was not front page news. Even if it had been, it was the type of story that people would read and think to themselves: *it's her own fault.*

Emily was not going to let that happen.

She made her way down the street, her head crowded with morose thoughts.

"Where are you?" she whispered.

Damien Harris knew. She was sure of it. She couldn't wait for Officer Andrews to find the time to track him down. What if Becky was in danger? Every wasted minute could be hurting her.

Emily quickened her pace. If she found Damien, what then? What if he was responsible for Becky's strange disappearance?

She didn't have to wait long to find out.

7

THE SUN WAS still bright, the sky still blue, but there was a darkness in Emily's heart as she walked home. Turning a corner onto a quieter road, the traffic disappeared. Shops were replaced by suburban homes, a line of white houses with red roofs. Children played out in the street. It was strange, she thought, how the world continues despite the horrors within it.

Her thoughts momentarily turned inward. In just a few weeks, a new chapter of her life would begin. But where would it start? She very much wanted to travel, to see the world.

Growing up in that tiny, non-descript village, she'd never gone anywhere. Her mother had said they could not afford holidays. She was a single parent raising a child in difficult times. That was true, but Emily also knew her mother found it difficult venturing out into the village, never mind an entirely different part of the world.

She didn't want to be like her mother. She wanted to go to new places, to explore new cultures, to embrace the unfamiliar.

If living independently for the last four years had taught her anything, it was that she no longer had to be the quiet, anxious girl who had wandered alone in playgrounds and hurried straight home from school.

But how was she going to explain it to her mother? At first, she had barely coped with only seeing Emily at weekends. When Emily had eventually whittled her visits down to every other weekend, her mother had withdrawn a little further.

She hadn't been home for over a month now. She felt guilty for it but she would be lying if she didn't also feel relief. How would her mother react to the news that her daughter was going to accept a job at High Mount Secondary School and remain in Somerset? Or that she was going to disappear for a year and travel the world. It was the kind of news that would tip her mother over the edge.

Her head heavy on her shoulders, Emily walked on. She was so engrossed in miserable thoughts that she didn't notice the black BMW convertible crawling behind her.

Was it her fate? To return to the village where nothing ever happened, and change was feared? She still had a few friends there. And her mother, of course. Plus, Lewis Hemmingway was still sending occasional and flirtatious text messages, alluding that she was 'the one that got away.' But what about teaching? What about seeing the world?

Emily shook the thoughts from her mind. She became aware of the low rumble of a car engine.

She stopped still, eyes fixed on the black BMW, which was pulling up beside her.

Her first instinct was to run. Her feet betrayed her, cementing themselves to the ground.

She watched as the driver window descended. Damien Harris sat behind the wheel. Emily was immediately struck by how handsome he was—square jaw, full lips, soft brown eyes that gave him an air of vulnerability. She had not expected that. In her mind, all drug dealers were pasty and scarred and unhealthy looking. Damien's attractiveness was disarming. Dangerous.

"You're Emily, right?" Damien said, his voice smooth with a trace of a local accent. He stared, his eyes fixed on hers; a hunter studying his prey.

Emily tried to take a step back but her legs refused to move.

"How… How do you know that?" Now her voice was betraying her, too.

Damien shrugged, even though his expression said he knew full well. "I hear you've been asking questions about me. Saying things…"

Down the street, children continued to play with a football. Emily gripped the straps of her bag. Her mind made a quick inventory of its contents, trying to find something that would serve as a weapon.

"Cat got your tongue?" Damien smiled, flashing perfectly aligned teeth. "Why are the police looking for me?"

"It's Becky…" Emily managed to stammer. "Becky Briar. She's missing."

"Never heard of her."

The smile remained but now there was a glint of something dark and dangerous in his eyes. Emily didn't dare look away.

"Becky's been missing since Monday night. If you know where she is…"

"I told you, I don't know her."

A young couple were approaching, holding hands and deep in conversation. They hadn't yet noticed Emily or the BMW.

"You were seen on Monday evening, arguing with Becky. She got into the car with you and you drove away."

"Who saw me?" Damien leaned toward the window. "Was it you?"

The couple had reached the car. Their conversation quietened as they passed by, first eyeing Emily and then Damien.

When they were out of earshot, Damien said, "Why don't you get in the car? We can talk in private."

Emily stared at the empty passenger seat. "No thank you."

"I don't know what you think you saw, but it isn't what you think."

"Where is she?"

"I'm not having this conversation in the street." He nodded to the empty seat beside him. "I promise to be good."

Emily stared at her feet, willing them to move. "You need to talk to the police. Tell them what you know."

"Me? Talk to the pigs? Why would I do that?"

"Because if you don't and something happens to Becky, the first person they'll suspect is you."

Emily's heart was pounding. The longer she stayed in his presence, the more afraid she felt.

Damien laughed. "And I'll tell them I don't know anything. That whoever it was that thought they saw me is mistaken. Tamara will back me up. She'll tell them I was with her all evening."

The smile returned to his lips; only this time it had a sharp edge.

Emily's throat was dry. She swallowed hard. "Maybe there was more than one eyewitness." It wasn't true, of course. But Becky was missing and here was the man who she'd last been seen with, lying through his teeth. It made her angry, even if that anger was quickly snuffed out by fear.

Damien's eyes narrowed. His smile was gone.

"I don't need the pigs sniffing around my business," he said. "I'm not going to prison because of that stupid bitch."

Emily winced. She hated the word.

"What happened?" she asked, her voice a whisper. She looked down the street. The young couple were just a smudge in the distance.

"Get in the car. We'll talk," Damien said. Emily did not move. "I won't hurt you, that's not my style. I just want the pigs off my back."

As if to show her his intentions, he switched off the engine and removed the keys from the ignition.

"We'll do a deal. I'll tell you where Becky went if you tell your friends in blue you were mistaken. It wasn't me you saw."

Emily hesitated. Her eyes returned to the empty seat.

"Time's ticking, Emily." Damien leaned across the car and popped open the passenger door.

Shit! Emily thought. She took a step forward.

"Give me the keys," she said. *What was she doing?* "Give me the keys and I'll get in. Only for a minute."

Damien stared at her with a raised eyebrow. He broke into a blinding grin.

"I knew I'd like you. Under that boring exterior, you take no shit."

He dangled his car keys between thumb and finger and held them out.

Ignoring the voice shrieking in her ear, Emily plucked the keys from his hand and stepped off the pavement.

56

Taking one last look around, she opened the passenger door and got in.

The interior of the car was decked out in chrome and black leather. A hula girl figurine sat on the dashboard in no mood to dance. Emily had expected the car to reek of marijuana, but the only smell to invade her nostrils was Damien's cologne. Sitting so close to him was unnerving; much like, she imagined, sitting next to a coiled snake. Afraid, she eyed the door, her only means of escape. If he tried anything, she would throw his keys and make a run for it.

"Don't freak out." Damien said. "You're safe with me." He stared at her with unblinking eyes.

Emily looked away. "What do you know?"

"I didn't hurt her. I know that's what you're thinking. I didn't touch a hair on her damn head." He leaned back a little, looking off into the distance. "Becky owes me money."

"For drugs?"

"Yes, officer. For drugs. She owed me for a long time, kept borrowing and promising she'd pay tomorrow. Tomorrow never came. Her debt kept mounting. I told her enough was enough, I wanted my money. She was supposed to bring it to me on Monday. The dumb cow turned up empty handed."

"So, you threatened her." Emily shot him a glare.

"I was pissed off, pretty unsurprising given the situation. I may have said some things, but I don't make threats lightly."

Emily felt her body inching away from his. Perhaps getting into the car had been a mistake.

Damien ran a hand over his cropped hair. "She told me she could get me the money that night but she needed a ride. I had plans with Tamara but I wanted my money. So, I gave her a ride. Thanks for telling Tamara all about that, by the way. She's now ignoring me."

"From what I hear, you'll recover." She risked a glance out of the window. Across the street, a cat crawled along a wall. A woman walked by with bags of shopping. "Where did you take her?"

"A few miles from here. Out in the countryside. I didn't see the house. I only saw the gate. It was one of those big ones that usually come with mansions. Becky told me to wait there in the car, that it wouldn't work if I showed up with her. She promised she'd be back in ten minutes. She walked to the gates, someone buzzed her through. That was the last time I saw her."

"What do you mean?"

"I mean the bitch didn't come back out. I called her phone but she didn't pick up. I even got out and buzzed the gates. No one answered. The stupid bitch pulled a fast one on me."

A flash of anger shot through Emily's body. "Can you please stop using that word?"

Damien bowed his head. "Yes, ma'am."

"She didn't tell you who lived there?"

"No. I waited. But I had places to be. I told myself I'd get that bi— I'd catch up with her the next day."

"What about an address?"

"She put it in the Sat Nav." He tapped the device on the dashboard.

Emily's mind raced. Who did Becky know that lived behind private gates in the countryside?

58

"You may have been the last person to see Becky before she disappeared," she said. "You need to tell the police what you've told me."

"You think I'm going to walk into a pig station and tell them what me and Becky fought about, just so they can arrest me? No fucking way."

"But the house…she could still be there. What if she's being held against her-"

Before Emily could finish the sentence, Damien leaned across the car and placed a hand on her shoulder. She flinched, pushing up against the door.

"Now, you listen to me," he said, his voice low and deliberate. "The only reason I told you anything is because I don't want the pigs breathing down my neck. That means you tell them you were mistaken—it wasn't me fighting with Becky that night. It was someone else. You want to check out that place, fine. I'll even give you the address. But you didn't get it from me. Understand?"

He was close enough now that Emily could feel his breath on her face. Somewhere outside, she heard laughter. A car drove past and was gone.

"I don't want to get anyone into trouble," she whispered. "I just want to find my friend."

"And I just want my money." Damien stared at her for a long time, his gaze moving from her eyes to her mouth. Slowly, he returned to his side of the car. "Mention my name to the police and you will regret it. I'm not a bad guy but I have a business to protect. I want Becky found. I want my money. Do we have an agreement?"

Emily nodded.

He reached for the Sat Nav and switched it on.

"Becky's not your friend, by the way," he said, searching

for the address. "She's no one's friend. Not even her own."

He showed Emily the Sat Nav screen and with a trembling hand, she tapped the address into her phone.

"Now be a good girl and run along," Damien said. He didn't look at her again, even when she threw his car keys into his lap. "Remember our agreement. I wouldn't want anyone else to get hurt."

Emily climbed out of the car and stepped onto the pavement. She watched Damien roll up his window, start the engine, and pull away. Only when the BMW had disappeared into the distance did she allow herself to breathe again. Her body trembled. Her heart hammered in her chest.

"You're an idiot, Emily Swanson," she said. "A dangerous, reckless idiot."

But she had a lead. She stared at the address on her phone screen. The question was, what did she do with it?

8

BECKY

THE FIRST THING she sensed as she came into consciousness was the metallic taste in her mouth. This was followed by a sudden and desperate thirst. She hadn't yet opened her eyes and, for a minute, she lay somewhere between the world of the living and the world of dreams. She had been falling into a bottomless void, surrounded by infinite blackness. It had been a strange dream. A frightening one. And yet, there had been something oddly soothing about disappearing.

Now that her body was beginning to wake, a chill teased goosepimples to her flesh; strange, since it was the beginning of summer. Just five more minutes, she thought. Five more minutes and I'll get up. The dream called to her, gently tugging at the edges of her mind. She could feel herself drifting off once more, into that inky nowhere space. She let her body be taken. She was falling again.

And then there was a voice, short and sharp, in her ear. *It's not a dream!*

Becky Briar opened her eyes. She blinked twice and groaned. It was still dark. The house was silent. Craving more sleep, she attempted to roll onto her side. Her body would not move. She shivered again. Why was it so damn cold? She reached for her duvet. It wasn't there. She must've kicked it off during her sleep. If she wasn't so damn tired, she would roll over and grab it from the floor. But she'd never felt so exhausted. And she was thirsty.

She swallowed, trying to produce saliva. The pain was excruciating, like swallowing broken glass.

Becky moaned. Then she noticed something. Her eyes had been open for at least thirty seconds now and they still hadn't accustomed themselves to the dark. In fact, all she could see was darkness. No shapes. No shadows or silhouettes.

Rolling her head to the left, she checked the time on her radio alarm clock. The clock was gone. Still half asleep, she reached out her hand. White hot pain shot through her limb, from her fingers to her shoulder.

Becky screamed but no sound came out. Any trace of the dream was gone. She sat bolt upright. All at once, fresh pain attacked her body, forcing her back down. A terrible ache began to pulse at the back of her head.

An image flashed in her mind. A shadow cutting through light.

Lying on her back, pain tearing at her, Becky tried to cry. No tears came.

I am not in my bed, she thought. *I am not in my room. This is not my house.*

Panic came, quickly eclipsed by blind terror. She tried to move her left hand again and was rewarded with more agony. She tried her right and found it in good working order. Her fingers scrabbled along the ground, searching for clues.

The ground was hard and icy cold. Now she had two

clues to her whereabouts: concrete and absolute darkness.

An overwhelming urge to cry out seized her. If her throat hadn't been so dry and if fear hadn't clamped her teeth together, she would have gladly obliged. Instead, she took deep, trembling breaths and waited for the nausea she was now feeling to pass. When she could focus again, she pushed herself up on her right arm, rolled onto her knees, and tried to stand. Her left arm swinging limply by her side, she staggered to her feet.

This time she did scream. Pain shot from her left ankle and up to her hip, exploding in a million white stars. She skittered forward, half hopping, half falling. The ground came up to meet her. She hit it hard and rolled.

Darkness took her once more.

Pain woke her. She didn't know how long she'd been unconscious. She waited a minute, fresh terror fighting the desire to sleep. Memories, muddled and fractured, danced in front of her. A car parked under a street lamp. Someone hiding in the shadows.

What had happened to her? Why couldn't she remember? Come to that, what *could* she remember?

My name is Becky Briar. I'm 22 years old. Life sucks.

Another voice whispered in her ear. It terrified her. *Sleep. Let it all go. Let the darkness wrap around you.*

Becky's body trembled. It was the darkness she feared the most. Was this what it was like to be blind? She couldn't stand it. She had to find a way out of here.

Using her good hand, she checked her body. She was wearing clothes (*thank God*): a light cotton jacket and beneath it some sort of blouse. On her legs, she wore jeans. She found two objects in the front right pocket. The first, to her relief, was her mobile phone. She'd call the police and get them to trace the call, or whatever they did, and come get her. She tapped the screen. When it didn't light up, she tried the power button. The battery was dead.

The second object in her pocket was a disposable lighter.

Pushing up into a seated position, Becky attempted to gain control of her trembling fingers. She took a deep breath and pushed her thumb down on the spark wheel. The room lit up in a flash. It was not enough time for her brain to register what her eyes were seeing. She tried again. And again. Eyes stinging, she tried for a fourth time. Sparks turned into a flame. The flame flickered and threatened to extinguish. Becky reached her left hand to cover it and was rewarded with more searing pain. In the weak light of the flame, she could see her left wrist was swollen to twice its normal size. Two of her fingers were bent at unnatural angles.

Slowly, she twisted her body from side to side. The ground beneath her was indeed concrete, and it was cracked in places and spotted with moss. She held the lighter out to her right. The ground stretched out beyond the reach of the flame. She could see no walls. She held the lighter above her head. She could see no ceiling, only darkness. Blood pulsed in Becky's ears. Where the hell was she?

For a moment, she wondered if she was outside, left for dead in wasteland on a starless night. But the air was musty. There were no night-time sounds.

There were no sounds at all.

Becky shivered. The flame flickered and died.

Plunged into darkness again, she resisted the urge to scream. She was still unbearably thirsty. Her body was a carcass of aches and pains. And now her head was floating away from her body.

Suddenly, she knew two things. If she didn't find water soon, she would die—and if she couldn't escape this impenetrable darkness, she would die.

Squeezing her eyes shut, she focused on her breathing and pushed the thoughts from her mind.

After what could have been five minutes or maybe an hour, Becky pushed herself up onto her knees once more.

She stood. Fresh pain shot through her left ankle.

Clenching her teeth, she applied more pressure. Perhaps her ankle wasn't broken after all. At the very least, she was suffering from a severe sprain. But she was standing. Her next feat was to try and walk.

Sparking up the lighter again, Becky held the flame up to the darkness and cast her body in a circle of protective light.

Catching her breath, fighting the pain, she hobbled forward.

9

ANGELA JACKSON WAS deeply unhappy. She sat behind the wheel, lips sealed together, brow pulled over worried eyes. She had barely spoken a word since Emily had shown up at her house and begged her to drive her out to the countryside. She had refused at first. She had too much work to be getting on with for tomorrow's class. And besides, she wanted nothing more to do with drug dealers and their psychotic girlfriends. But when Emily mentioned Damien was demanding to know who'd seen him that night, a chord of terror was struck. Emily felt guilty about it, but a little intimidation had done the trick.

Now, the town was dwindling in the rear-view mirror, tangerine sunset painting the roofs, as the VW headed into the countryside. A few minutes later and they were passing fields of corn, maize, and rape. The scene reminded Emily of home, and for a second, her mind wandered back to the choices she still had to make.

"I'm sorry for dragging you into this," she said. "Charlotte wasn't home and you're the only other person I know with a car."

Angela was quiet, her eyes on the road. "I still don't understand why we're out here. Shouldn't you be passing this information onto the police?"

"I will. I just want to see if Damien was telling the truth."

Damien's threats echoed in Emily's head. The truth was that she did believe him. It was the police force she was having difficulty with. They were taking too long. Among the crimes they were currently investigating, Becky's disappearance was not a priority. It was a small station. Why spend limited resources looking for someone who had probably skipped town, when there were serious crimes to be dealt with? But Emily didn't believe Becky had skipped town. She had no evidence, just a feeling in her gut. If there was something at this address that could prove Becky was in trouble, surely the police had to respond.

The robotic voice of the Sat Nav instructed Angela to turn left. She spun the wheel, turning off the road and onto a narrow lane, passing a sign that read: PRIVATE ROAD. Hedges grew up on both sides, followed by an archway of trees. The evening light was plunged into shadows. Angela's grip on the steering wheel tightened.

"This must be it," Emily said. "Pull up over here."

Angela slowed the car to a halt. A short distance away, a pair of wrought iron gates stood between two granite pillars.

Emily peered through the passenger window. The gates were impressive: black and towering, with an ornate crest welded at the top. Two lions, reared up on their hind legs, faced each other, while serpents writhed around their bodies. Beyond the gates, a wide gravel road curved sharply and disappeared into woodland.

"What was Becky doing out here?" Angela's wide eyes moved from the gate to the rear-view mirror.

It was a question Emily couldn't answer. According to Damien, Becky had entered those gates but hadn't returned.

Angela's voice interrupted her thoughts. "So, Damien was telling the truth. Let's go. I'll drive you to the police station, but I'm not coming in. I know I'm a pushover, Emily, but this is just too much."

Emily reached for the door handle.

"What are you doing?"

"Just a second."

Angela's eyes bulged in their sockets. "Emily, no! Did you listen to anything I just said? We need to go. Now!"

But Emily was already climbing out of the car.

"I'm just going to look through the gates, that's all. Just one look and then we can go."

Emily shut the door, and turning her back on the car, walked along the road. She could still hear Angela's complaints when she reached the gates. They were even more impressive up close. There were not only lions and serpents but also an intricate network of tree branches and leaves. Whoever had welded these gates was a master of their craft.

Emily wrapped her fingers around the bars. Apart from the rumble of the car engine, it was quiet. Not even birds sang in the trees. Stepping to the left, she cocked her head and strained to see beyond the bend. Whoever lived here, whatever lay beyond, privacy was clearly important. Which usually meant there was something to hide.

The gates were electronically locked. There was an intercom beside the left pillar and a plaque beside the right, which read: BEAUMONT HOUSE.

Taking out her phone, Emily snapped a picture. Peering back at the car, she held up a finger and mouthed, "One second." She could see Angela furiously shaking her head.

Emily stepped up to the intercom. Temptation stole into

her fingers. What if whoever lived there was Becky's friend? They could have helped her to get away from Damien. They could know where she was hiding out. *Becky could still be inside.* If that was the case, why hadn't she replied to any of Emily's calls or text messages? Another thought struck Emily as her finger hovered over the buzzer. What if Becky was still inside but was being held against her will?

Before she could stop herself, Emily pressed the buzzer. She waited, drumming her fingers against her thighs. Perhaps no one's home, she thought

She waited a few seconds more, looking up and down the tall dry-stone wall that ran the length of the road. Behind it, trees stood side by side like sentries, protecting whatever was inside. Emily didn't like it. She didn't like it one bit.

Angela was angrily signalling to her to return to the car. Emily stared through the gates, following the gravel road with her eyes until it disappeared. Her gaze moved back to the wall. It was climbable. She could take a quick look. Perhaps see what lay beyond the bend in the road. She could be in and out in two minutes.

Ignoring Angela's high-pitched voice, Emily walked along beside the wall. She came to a halt a few metres to the right of the gates. Finding a suitable foothold, she sucked in a breath. She began to climb.

10

TREES RAN THE length of the wall in a narrow strip. Weaving between them, Emily stepped out onto the gravel road. More trees flanked the other side. She stood for a second, glancing over her shoulder at the closed gates. Then, gravel crunching beneath her shoes, she walked on.

From here, the road stretched out in a straight line before veering to the left fifty metres up ahead. As Emily walked, she thought of Angela sitting out on the road. Guilt grew heavy on her shoulders. Angela was kind and sensitive, and desperate to please. She was the type of person who others took advantage of. Just as Emily had done this evening. She would apologise as soon as she returned to the car, and hope that Angela would still be talking to her tomorrow.

Emily reached the bend in the road. Uncertain of what lay beyond, she stepped off the gravel and into the trees. It was a wise move.

Ahead of her, the road opened into a wide gravel drive, where a handful of expensive looking cars were parked. Just beyond was a grand house built of yellow sandstone and capped by a slate roof. It was the type of house she'd seen in period dramas on television. The kind that had endless bedrooms and servant quarters in the attic.

Emily stood in shadows, enthralled by its grandeur. Who lived there? More importantly, was Becky inside?

Wondering what she should do, Emily contemplated her options. She could walk up to the house, knock on the door, and explain who she was and why she was here. Or she could remain hidden and watch for a while.

Taking out her phone, she switched to camera mode, zoomed in, and began snapping pictures of the house. Next, she took photographs of the cars. One of the vehicles stood out from the others. Unlike the classics, it was a modern five-door hatchback. She zoomed in further on the camera, taking fuzzy pictures of the license plates.

A flash of red caught her eye. The front door of the house had opened. Standing on the top step, wearing a bright red dress and a ribbon in her hair, was a young girl about eight years old. She was staring in the direction of the trees, her head swivelling from left to right.

Emily ducked behind a large trunk then peered out.

The girl was tall and thin, with straight, black hair and porcelain skin. A deep line creased the middle of her forehead. For a second, it was as if she was peering directly at Emily.

Emily held her breath, not daring to move. The girl descended the steps and began walking down the gravel road. She was just a few metres away now, her footsteps echoing in Emily's ears. She reached the edge of the trees and stopped. Swinging her shoulders from side to side, she peered into the shadows.

Emily contemplated stepping out from her hiding place. In her limited teaching experience, children always told the truth when it came to matters of importance. Perhaps this girl could tell her about Becky.

Before Emily could decide, a deep, commanding voice filled the air.

"Delia! What the bloody hell are you doing? Go back inside the house at once!"

The girl did not reply, but Emily heard her expel a deep sigh.

The voice came again, this time accompanied by fast and heavy footsteps. "Do not ignore me, Delia! I've had quite enough of your rubbish today. Go inside. Now."

Tendrils of musty cologne reached through the trees. Emily's heart began to pound.

"Do not defy me, girl. There's enough trouble in this house right now without you causing more."

The girl emitted a mouse-like squeal. Her feet skittered and dragged through the gravel.

"Where's your bloody mother, anyway?" The voice was moving back toward the house.

Sucking in a deep breath, Emily poked her head out from behind the tree.

The man was tall and broad, with a thick head of greying hair, and he was dressed in an expensive suit. His large hand gripped the girl's spindly arm as he dragged her back to the house like a rag doll. She was struggling to keep up, her feet lifting from the ground.

Anger boiled Emily's blood. She contemplated marching after him to deliver a lecture about the deep-seated effects of physical abuse, and she would have done so had she not been breaking all kinds of trespass laws.

The man was ascending the stone steps, the girl dangling from his hand. It was painful to watch. But then Emily had an idea.

Taking out her phone, she quickly took pictures of the

man's rough treatment of his daughter. As well as finding Becky, the police could investigate an abuse case.

The man and the girl had reached the top of the stairs. Somebody else was coming out of the house. But it was not the girl's mother. It was another man. A man who, even from this distance, Emily instantly recognised.

Stopping to talk to the man in the suit was Emily's lecturer, Bill Creed. She watched as Bill stooped to pat the girl on the head and plant a kiss on her forehead. The girl ran inside, pausing in the doorway to look back at the men. When she was gone, the two began to talk.

Emily's heart raced. She could not hear what they were saying but neither could she move any closer without detection. Instead, she observed their body language. The man was at least a head taller than Bill. He leaned over him, one hand on his hip, the other stabbing a finger at the house. Bill stood with folded arms. His spine was stiff, his shoulders taut. It wasn't an argument, Emily thought. But both men appeared deeply concerned.

What was Bill doing here? Not two days ago, he had sat behind his desk and told Emily he hadn't seen Becky in weeks. Something was wrong. She could feel it in the pit of her stomach, crawling like insects. Lifting her phone once more, she snapped pictures of Bill and the man. They shook hands. Bill made his way down the steps and toward the hatchback.

Transfixed, Emily watched as he started the engine. The man in the suit lifted a hand. Bill manoeuvred the car onto the gravel road. It was then Emily remembered Angela was still waiting outside.

Her body sprang to life. The car rolled toward her. Emily leapt back, ducking behind the tree just as Bill passed by. His eyes were fixed on the road ahead. A fleeting glance confirmed to Emily that he was not a happy man. Regardless of his mood, he was going to make it to the gates before Emily would reach the wall.

Angela answered after one ring. "Emily, where the hell are you? I can't believe you left me here!"

"Listen, I don't have time to explain but you need to drive. Get out of there, Angela!"

"What are you talking-"

"Someone's coming your way right now. I don't want them to see you."

"But what about-"

"Angela Jackson do as your bloody told! I'll call you back in five minutes. And for your sake you better come back and get me!"

Angela squealed in her ear. Emily hung up. Seconds later, a car sped past on the other side of the wall, followed a minute a later by a second vehicle.

Bill Creed.

Glancing once more at the house, Emily turned and made her way back to the wall. She waited another three minutes before calling Angela again.

Once she had hoisted herself over the wall, she stood by the roadside, her thoughts tripping over each other as she watched for the VW.

11

BECKY

THE SPACE IN which Becky was imprisoned was huge. She'd been hobbling forward in what she thought was a straight line for over a minute now, her damaged arm swinging limply by her side. Yes, she was moving slowly, but even if she'd been crawling on her hands and knees, she should have reached a wall by now.

The darkness did not help matters. She had waited for her eyes to adjust, for shapes and shadows to present themselves.

But darkness remained, black and impenetrable.

She had used the lighter a few times, its weak flame revealing only more concrete, before the heat burned her fingers and blistered her skin.

Becky stopped for a second, pain and nausea threatening to topple her. Then she was on the move once more, one foot sort of in front of the other. Her injured ankle complained bitterly and hurt more each time she put weight on it. She could not stop, though. To stop would mean she would die.

She was beginning to lose hope, to believe that perhaps she had died and that she was stuck in an infinite chasm of purgatory, when her stomach bumped against something solid. Startled by the impact, she disturbed the silence with a strangled cry and stumbled backward, sending more pain shooting up her leg.

When she'd calmed herself, Becky reached out with her good hand and felt around. Corrugated metal chilled her fingertips. She moved her hand to the left and the metal disappeared, leaving her hand dancing in mid-air.

Pulling the lighter from her pocket, she pressed down on the spark wheel. A flame ignited.

She was standing in front of a kitchen sink. Rust covered its once chrome surface. Mould grew in the basin. She moved the lighter from left to right. The flame illuminated other objects: a dilapidated chest freezer; a broken chair lying on its side; a refrigerator in the corner, its door ripped off and face down on the ground. Becky turned ninety degrees. By some sort of miracle, she had passed straight through an open doorway into what had once been a kitchen.

Confusion creased her brow. *What is this place?*

She was beginning to suspect she was somewhere underground. There were no windows. No indication of light anywhere. Just unending, tomb-like darkness.

Eyeing the sink in the flickering light, she ran her shrivelled tongue over parched lips. Slipping the lighter into her back pocket, she let the darkness envelop her. She reached out a hand, fumbling around until she found the taps. She tried the first. It had rusted, and refused to budge. She tried the second. After some effort, the tap handle shifted. Hope caught in Becky's throat. She waited for the sweet sound of water splashing on steel. She heard only silence.

She waggled her fingers beneath the tap's spout. She pushed the handle in the opposite direction and tried again.

Nothing.

She was going to die. The realisation was as natural as drawing breath. It didn't matter whether it was her injuries or dehydration that got to her first; she was going to die and there was nothing she could do about it.

An urge to scream began to manifest. She clenched her teeth and swallowed it back down. If she screamed now, she knew she would not be able to stop.

But there was so much she had left to do! Like travel the world and not make an entire mess of her life. Like…

Becky slumped against the sink. An image lit up her mind. It was brief, lasting no more than a half second, but the violence it depicted left a bloody stain. She saw a hand gripping a crowbar. Her arms, crossed over her face. The crowbar crashing against her head. Pain, sweet and sharp. The ground, cold and wet. A light shining above her. A shadow cutting through it. The crowbar coming down again. Darkness.

Someone had tried to kill her.

But who? Her eyes searched the darkness for answers. She closed them, as if the action would help her to focus. Another image flashed before her. It was night. She was walking across deserted wasteland, to a car parked in the shadows. Someone was standing by the car, waiting for her…

The image disappeared. Becky's grip on the sink tightened.

You have to remember.

Someone had brought her here and left her to die in this underground prison. That meant there was a way in and out. All she had to do was find it.

"Okay," Becky breathed into the darkness.

Retrieving the lighter, she sparked it up. She glanced longingly at the rusted sink then examined the rest of the room once more.

Something caught her eye. Along from the refrigerator, there was a poster on the wall. She hobbled up to it, biting down on her lip as fresh pain threatened to send her back to the ground. She came closer.

Letters swam into focus and began forming words. Becky bit down harder.

In the flickering flame, she read the fading words at the top of the poster: IN CASE OF EMERGENCY.

Below, was a diagram of her prison. It was a strange design: a large circular chamber sat in the centre, with six smaller rooms running off it, connected by corridors. Like a wheel, Becky thought.

A series of labels and instructions relayed protocols for various emergencies. In the case of fire, fire extinguishers and fire blankets could be found in designated areas: the kitchen, all sleeping quarters, storage rooms A and C, and to the right of both the main entrance and the emergency escape ladder.

To Becky's surprise and delight, the main entrance was situated just to the right of the kitchen. The emergency escape ladder was in the north-east section of the central chamber. She quickly counted the corridors that lay in between the kitchen and the ladder. There were three.

The smell of burning flesh tore Becky from her thoughts. Wincing, she dropped the lighter and sucked her blistering thumb.

Darkness enveloped her once more. This time, terror

did not have such a tight grip. Adrenaline was surging through her body, firing her synapses.

She could escape from here. The main entrance was just metres away. If it was impenetrable, she could try for the ladder. There was a question of how she would climb the ladder in her current state, but she would answer it when the time came.

Using the wall as leverage, she slid down into a crouch, wiped away phantom tears of pain, and fumbled around.

Two minutes later, the lighter was back in her hand. The pain in her ankle had grown worse. Perhaps it was a fracture. Was it possible to walk on a fractured ankle? She wasn't sure. But if she was going to escape from here, she was going to need both feet on the ground and moving one in front of the other.

Pushing herself back up the wall, Becky sparked the lighter. A small flame ignited. It grew small and died. She sparked the lighter again, bursting the blister on her thumb. She could not get it to light again.

Terror clambered up her body.

Lie down, the darkness whispered. *Sleep. Dream. Let it all float away.*

The voice was soothing. It made her want to shut her eyes. But she couldn't. She would die.

Burning the image of the map into her mind, Becky drew in a ragged breath and held it until her lungs felt as if they would burst. Letting it out, she pressed her shoulder gently against the wall, and limped forward.

12

FRIDAY

THE MORNING BROUGHT warm showers and a blue grey sky. Emily woke at 6:30 AM and set about marking classwork that should have been taken care of the previous night. She was in a foul mood, in part, thanks to Officer Andrews. After leaving Beaumont House, an infuriated Angela had taken Emily to the local police station and, in no uncertain terms, had told her not to call again until the finals were over. Only then might she consider rekindling their friendship. Emily was hurt but she understood.

At the police station, Officer Andrews was finally available to speak. Emily had suddenly found herself hesitant to share the details of her findings. She would be exposing Becky's drug habit to the law, and she was worried about the consequences. As for Damien Harris, she had deliberated whether she should tell Officer Andrews the full details of his involvement, but how could she explain the rest of the story without revealing his role? If the police chose to investigate his criminal activities, that was of his own doing, not hers.

Officer Andrews had sat and listened to Emily's recount with mounting concern. He looked at the photographs she'd snapped at Beaumont House, taking particular interest in the images of a father roughly handling his daughter. When Emily had finished, Officer Andrews began a long lecture on the dangers of taking police matters into her own hands. Getting into the car of a drug dealer— one who was possibly connected to the disappearance of a young woman—was not only dangerous but incredibly naive. As for trespassing on private property and taking candid photographs without her subjects' knowledge, Emily was putting both Officer Andrews and the police establishment in a difficult position.

"Leave the police work to the police," Officer Andrews said. "You're putting yourself and my investigation at risk."

Emily countered by saying she couldn't see much of an investigation going on, and then reminded him that Becky had now been missing for more than three days. Officer Andrews responded by asking the desk sergeant to arrange for a cab to take Emily home.

Now, as she rode the bus to High Mount Secondary School, Emily's frustration ran deep. What did Bill Creed have to do with any of this? And who was the man from Beaumont House? Officer Andrews had reacted as if he'd recognised him but would say no more on the matter. All Emily could do now was get on with her day and hope Officer Andrews got in touch soon.

She stared out the window, watching the morning traffic and stifling a yawn. She was running on four hours' sleep with a full day of teaching ahead. In just over two weeks, her studies would be over. Providing she passed the final exams, she would be a qualified teacher. Principal Talbot's offer of staying on at High Mount still loomed over her. She would need to decide very soon.

But not today.

As if Emily's mother had a window into her thoughts, a text message popped up on her phone screen.

Where are you? I tried calling last night but you didn't answer. I'm worried. Please call and tell me you're all right.

A headache brewing, Emily sent a quick reply, reassuring her mother that her only child was not lying dead in a ditch. She regretted the joke instantly as images of Becky doing exactly that flashed in her head. She sent another text, promising to call on her lunch hour.

No sooner had she sent it her phone began to ring.

"Not now, Mother," Emily groaned.

But it was not her mother calling.

"Good morning Ms Swanson, this is Evelyn Peters, Vice Chancellor Eriksson's PA. The Vice Chancellor would like to see you as a matter of some urgency. Could you come in this afternoon, at four-thirty?"

"What's this about?" Anxiety fluttered in Emily's stomach. She'd never spoken to Vice Chancellor Eriksson before, let alone received a call requesting her company. Judging by Evelyn Peters' tone of voice this wasn't to be a social visit.

"I wouldn't have the faintest idea," the PA said. "Should I tell him to expect you?"

Emily hesitated. Had Officer Andrews already been in touch with Bill Creed? Surely, he hadn't had the time. The anxiety in her stomach tumbled and flipped, giving way to dread. It had to be about Becky. Was Vice Chancellor Eriksson going to deliver bad news?

"I'll be there," Emily's croaked, her voice a whisper.

"Very good."

The PA hung up, leaving Emily staring out the bus

window, a hundred terrible thoughts racing through her mind.

Please, no, she thought.

13

BECKY

SHE'D MADE IT out of the kitchen but the pain in her ankle was becoming unbearable. The only way she was moving was by leaning hard into the wall with her left shoulder and then lurching forward while putting her weight on her right foot. Occasionally, she slipped and her weight shifted to her left foot. The pain felt like glass tearing through bone, flesh, and sinew. If she lost her balance, Becky knew she would not get up again.

According to the map, the main entrance to this strange underground building should be coming up on her left any minute now. Becky pushed forward, refusing to stop even though she needed to catch her breath.

She was about to succumb to panic when the wall suddenly vanished. She skittered to the left. Her injured foot and ankle taking the full force of her body. Becky screamed. Her shoulder slammed into metal with a dull thud. She spun a half-turn and before she could fight it, gravity dragged her toward the ground.

Her hand shot up. Fingers wrapped around metal bars and held on tight.

Somehow, she had stopped herself from falling. Her

good leg had shot straight out and pushed her weight against the metal. Her working hand had done the rest.

Chest heaving, she hoisted herself up and turned around. She was holding onto some sort of wheel. She leaned forward, pressing her face against icy metal.

She'd reached the main doors. This was her way out.

Fresh adrenaline pumped through her veins as she examined the wheel. It had to be the door's opening mechanism, like the ones found on ships.

All she had to do now was get it open.

And then what?

She had no idea what lay on the other side. What if she found herself miles from help? She'd been down here for—hours, a day, two days?—drifting in and of consciousness. She was severely injured and dehydrated. What if help wasn't on the other side of that door? She recalled with unsettling clarity an article she had once read about how long a person could survive without food and water. With nothing to eat, she would be able to survive for weeks, so long as she had water. But without water…four, maybe five days at most.

She took a moment to listen to her body. To *feel* it. She didn't need to be an expert to tell she didn't have long. A day, maybe two.

Clamping her jaw, Becky pushed deathly thoughts from her mind and gripped the door wheel. She pulled herself up until she was standing. Pain wracked her body, followed by a wave of nausea. Above her ragged breaths, she thought she heard a voice calling her name. She held her breath and listened. The voice did not come again.

Becky tightened her grip on the wheel and turned. The wheel did not budge. She rested for a few seconds and tried again, this time using more force. The wheel shifted to the left. Just by a centimetre. But it had moved.

Adrenaline filled her veins and her heart as she tried again.

No matter how much force she applied, the wheel would not turn any further.

Becky stood holding onto it, as if letting go would be to let go of hope. But she was too weak. Too exhausted. Slumping against the door, she let her hand fall to her side. Hopelessness embraced her. Why was this happening to her? Who could do something so cruel? What had she done to deserve this?

Her mind flashed with another memory. Like a freight train, the events of that night came hurtling through the dark.

She walks toward the car, past weeds and litter and discarded shopping trolleys. The ground is hard beneath her feet. Somewhere behind, a sound rumbles through the air, followed by the screech of metal and the hiss of steam. She sees a figure standing motionless in the shadows. She feels eyes upon her.

"You're late," she tells the figure. "You were supposed to be here already."

The figure's voice is low, angry. "You didn't give me much time."

"You brought everything I asked for?"

The figure hesitates then opens the back door of the car. A bag is retrieved and thrown at Becky's feet.

"Steady," Becky says. "You're lucky I didn't ask you to bring more of my money."

"It's not your money. It's mine. You have no right to take it from me."

Becky is a metre away from the car. Close enough to hear breaths pumping in and out. Everything blurs and turns black. There is a hole in this memory. Pieces of it have been torn out.

"I'll be gone soon," she hears herself saying. She is back by the car. Time has moved on. "This will all be over."

The figure reaches into the shadows.

"I know." Light glances off metal as the figure raises a hand high into the air. "Good riddance."

There's not even time to scream.

Becky sucked in a gasp of cold air. Suddenly, she knew who had attacked her. She knew who had left her to rot down here with no chance of rescue.

And she knew why they had done it, too. She had deserved it.

She was going to die down here.

Escape lay inches on the other side of the door like a cruel punchline to a bad joke. But she was going to die. She deserved to. All the terrible things she'd done had finally colluded with the fates to make her pay.

Anger welled inside. *Screw them,* she thought. Maybe she deserved to be down here but she wasn't the most terrible person in the world. There were people out there— monsters—who were capable of far more heinous acts. She'd been given a bad hand to play with, that was all. To win with a bad hand, you have to play a little dirty.

Becky's knees trembled beneath her. If she was going to give up, now was the time. Just sit down and wait for madness or dehydration to finish her off. It would be easy. Let the feet go. Let the back slide. She could close her eyes and succumb to the whispers that were growing louder in her ear with each passing minute.

Sit down and wait to die.

Or hang onto a remaining thread of hope.

Because there *was* one last thread to grasp before she gave up: the emergency escape ladder.

The idea of it made her laugh out loud. The laughter made her throat burn. She pictured herself attempting to climb a ladder in pitch blackness, with a broken hand and a fucked up ankle, not to mention the nausea and dizziness that were coming in frequent waves.

Or the fact that she was starting to hear things.

Like the dripping sound she could hear now—there was no way in hell it could be real.

It was certainly doing a good impression of sounding real. Becky cocked her head and listened. It was the same sound, repeated over and over, coming from somewhere in the darkness of the chamber. It was unmistakable: the sound of water splashing on metal. The sound made her internal organs contract with yearning. Had the sound always been there? Why was she only noticing it now?

"Because it's not real," she croaked.

The emergency escape ladder *was* real. It was located three corridors to the left of the kitchen. Or was it two? All she had to do was retrace her steps, count the corridors as she felt her way along the wall, and hope she had the strength left to make it to the ladder. She didn't hold out much hope that she could climb the damn thing. But she had to try. Even if it was the last thing she did.

She laughed again. She sounded insane.

"Get rich or die trying," she croaked. "Go hard or go home."

Pushing away from the door, Becky hovered for a second, swaying dangerously back and forth.

Three corridors. Or was it two?

Dragging one foot in front of the other, Becky headed back in the direction of the kitchen, the fingers of her good hand brushing against the wall.

14

ARRIVING AT THE campus a little before 4:30, Emily headed straight to Vice Chancellor Eriksson's office. Evelyn Peters greeted her with a curt smile and asked her to take a seat in the waiting area. She spoke in a hushed voice on the phone then informed Emily that the Vice Chancellor would see her in just a few minutes.

While she waited, Emily attempted to steady her breathing, which had become uneven and shallow. Her feet tapped on the ground. She felt as if she was back at school waiting to see the principal. Not that she had ever been called to the principal's office more than once, and that had not been due to bad behaviour but because her mother had been going through a particularly anxious phase, giving the school cause for concern. That meeting had resulted in the one and only visit Emily and her mother had received from the local social worker.

Why was she thinking about that now?

Evelyn Peters' phone rang. The PA nodded in Emily's direction.

"You can go in now. They're waiting for you."

Blood rushed in Emily's ears. *They?*

Muttering a thank you to the PA, she made her way past the reception desk and to the Vice Chancellor's office door.

Knocking softly, she sucked in a breath.

A deep, rumbling voice told her to come in. Emily did as she was told. It took just a few seconds to absorb the scene.

Vice Chancellor Eriksson sat behind a great oak desk, his eyes fixed on Emily as she entered. He was a large, imposing man who was in good shape, with thick blond hair, and an expression that chilled Emily to the bone.

As her gaze shifted to the left, she instantly knew why she was here. Sat in an armchair by the window was her lecturer Bill Creed. If his presence was not enough to convince Emily that she was in trouble, the man standing next to him hammered in the nails.

It was the man from Beaumont House.

He turned and glared at Emily as she moved into the room. Now she could get a closer look, she saw he was in his early fifties with sharp features and hawk-like eyes. He was dressed in another expensively tailored suit, and that same cologne he'd worn back at the house now permeated the room.

Emily stopped still. Her heart hammered as her eyes moved from man to man.

"Please take a seat, Emily."

She moved to the empty chair at the desk and sat down.

"I don't believe we've had the pleasure of meeting before," Vice Chancellor Eriksson said, his voice calm and steady, "but Bill here tells me good things about you. He says you'll make an excellent teacher."

Across the room, Bill was finding it difficult to meet Emily's gaze.

"Unfortunately, we're not here to talk about your talents as a teacher." Vice Chancellor Eriksson paused. It felt intentional, to make Emily feel more uncomfortable than she already did. "Do you know the gentleman standing in the window?"

Emily risked the quickest of glances at the man. He stared back at her. She shook her head.

"This is Councillor Timothy Beaumont, MP. He is quite a prominent figure both in local and national politics. He also happens to be a very generous philanthropist. He and his wife Sara are heavily involved in several charities and fundraising events. Councillor Beaumont also makes a generous annual donation to this university."

In the window, Councillor Beaumont was motionless and unsmiling.

Emily fixed her gaze on the desk. She could feel a roomful of eyes upon her, boring into her innermost thoughts.

Vice Chancellor Eriksson continued. "Perhaps you could explain to us, Emily, how you came to find yourself trespassing at Councillor Beaumont's home yesterday."

Emily was quiet, the realisation that this meeting had been set up to lambaste her sinking into her stomach like poison. It was intimidating to say the least, and surely against university policy. She risked a glance up at Vice Chancellor Eriksson. She'd never heard much about him. He was a distant figure, one wrapped up in administration and bureaucracy, and rarely involved in his students' everyday lives. This was not how she had expected their first meeting to go.

Their eyes locked across the table. Emily fought the urge to look away.

"I'm assuming the reason we're here is because you've spoken to Officer Andrews," she said, finding her voice at last although it was no more than a whisper, "So you'll already have the answer to your question."

A smile teased the corner of Vice Chancellor Eriksson's mouth.

Bill Creed spoke next. "Emily, I feel I need to explain something. I feel I haven't been entirely honest with you."

Emily folded her arms across her chest, which didn't help her breathing.

"As you recently learned, I received a phone call from the principal of Becky's school placement, saying she'd missed several sessions, enough to cause unwarranted disruption. I asked Becky to come and see me, which she did."

"You told me you weren't able to get hold of her."

"True. But this was before I learned she was missing." Bill pulled at his tie. "I spoke to Becky about my concerns. She admitted she was experiencing financial difficulties. As I understand it, she receives no support from her family, and with the soaring rate of university fees, the stress was beginning to take its toll. She was falling further and further behind, to the point where she was questioning if she should continue.

"We talked about finding work but with the amount of catching up she had to do, there was little time to fit in a part-time job that would inevitably pay a minimum wage. That's when I suggested coming to work for Tim—for Councillor Beaumont and his wife."

Emily's mouth hung open. If this were true, she had just learned more about Becky in two minutes than in an entire year of living with her. But was it true? For someone who had been suffering financial hardship, Becky certainly seemed able to afford a busy social life. Lately, she'd barely spent an evening at home. And what about the drugs? Emily had no idea but she assumed they didn't come free.

"Councillor Beaumont's wife is a good friend of my mother's," Bill continued. "I knew the Beaumonts were looking for help with their daughter, Delia, and so I put Becky in touch with them. Delia is autistic. I thought with Becky's teaching skills she would be a suitable candidate. I also knew she would be paid very well. At the time, it seemed like a perfect idea." Bill pulled at his tie again. "The reason I couldn't tell you this before is because Councillor Beaumont is an important man with access to classified government information. Becky was required to sign a non-disclosure agreement, forbidding her to tell people who she is employed by."

Emily's gaze switched to Councillor Beaumont. She recalled the way he had handled his daughter, which seemed even more abhorrent now that she had learned about Delia's needs.

"Things started off well," Bill said. "Councillor Beaumont reported that Delia and Becky had a good rapport. Sara was pleased with the level of support and empathy Becky could offer. And in turn, Becky was financially better off. I took the trouble to speak to her teaching placement on her behalf. Under the circumstances, they were happy for her to return as long as she could show a willing commitment. Things seem to be getting back on track for Becky. Until about a month ago."

Councillor Beaumont cleared his throat.

"Rebecca began to miss tutoring sessions," he said, his voice filled with a confidence borne from years of public speaking. "I don't know how much you are aware about autism, Ms Swanson, but routine and predictability are both crucial elements needed to keep everyone involved happy. The first time that Rebecca missed a session, Delia became very agitated and upset. When Delia becomes upset it can take a long time to calm her. It's very stressful for everyone. If I had been solely responsible for Rebecca's employment I would have terminated her contract immediately. But my wife is far more forgiving than I.

"When Rebecca called later that day, she was deeply apologetic, explaining there had been some sort of family crisis. We forgave her—she had been very reliable up until that point. However, although she was present the next few sessions, she was late each time. Then, she stopped coming altogether. We didn't hear from her. She would not reply to my wife's calls. Delia became increasingly difficult. We contacted Bill, who told us Rebecca had all but disappeared from her studies, and so my wife began to interview prospective new tutors. We did not expect to hear from Rebecca again. But on Monday evening, there she was, standing on our doorstep."

Councillor Beaumont's eyes darkened. "She wanted money. Can you believe that? A temporary loan, she said, which she promised to pay back as soon as she could. My wife and I were both shocked. It had to be some sort of joke. But Rebecca did not look well. She had lost weight since we'd last seen her. She was terribly pale. My wife suspected some sort of substance abuse. I suppose it would explain Rebecca's frequent absences and her dishevelled appearance that night. She told us she was leaving, that the money was to help her get home. She could not ask her parents as they had their own financial struggles. She said she had no one else to ask. No one else to turn to. And I suppose, knowing that we were financially comfortable and of a charitable nature, she assumed we would be able to help."

"How much money did she ask to borrow?" Emily asked.

"We didn't get that far," Councillor Beaumont said. "I refused to give her any sort of loan. The girl could not be relied upon to show up for paid employment, so how could I expect her to repay a loan? Besides, I'm not in the habit of funding drug addiction."

"You don't know that Becky has a drug habit."

"And yet, we've learned that she travelled to our house with a known drug dealer. Giving him our location. What if he'd planned to rob us? No, I was not about to lend money to a dropout who frequents with known criminals." He glanced across at Vice Chancellor Eriksson, who had been listening with his hands clasped in front of him. "Perhaps I behaved rashly that night. My wife certainly thought so. She gave Rebecca fifty pounds for the train fare and called her a cab to take her to the station. My wife waited with Rebecca until the cab came twenty minutes later. We didn't see her again."

Emily leaned forward. "And you didn't think to find out what kind of trouble she was in?"

Councillor Beaumont stared at her, open-mouthed.

"What about the taxi?" Emily said, directing the question at Bill. "Do we know where it actually took her?"

Across the desk, Vice Chancellor Eriksson cleared his throat. "Ms Swanson, we are not gathered here for you to conduct an interrogation. Quite the opposite, in fact. Trespass. Allegations of abuse. Insinuations that somehow Councillor Beaumont and Bill here had something to do with Miss Briar's disappearance." He stared over his desk. Emily felt very small then. Her hands began to tremble.

95

"It's clear to me what the truth is. Rebecca developed a drug habit, leading her to fail at her studies and to fall in with...some unscrupulous characters. Clearly, she got herself into some sort of trouble and has taken the next train out of town."

"She told Councillor Beaumont she was going home," Emily insisted. "She didn't make it."

"It was clearly a lie. A ruse to convince him to give her money."

Emily was shaking now. Not with fear, she realised, but with anger.

"You can choose to believe that Rebecca is in some kind of terrible peril," Eriksson said, "but facts are facts. As Officer Andrews' report concludes, Rebecca Briar is missing by choice. As an adult, she has a legal right to disappear. That is exactly what she's chosen to do."

Emily stared in disbelief from man to man.

"Officer Andrews' report?" she breathed. "What do you know about Officer Andrews' report?"

15

BECKY

SHE HAD ALREADY passed the kitchen and the first of the three corridors, almost falling into its fathomless, hungry mouth. For ten terrifying seconds, she lost touch with the wall and wandered blindly in the dark, left leg lurching beneath her, and with Death chasing her from behind. Only when her fingers glanced against the bricks did she feel safe again. It felt odd to feel safe down here when she was half dead and blinded by darkness. The feeling hadn't lasted for long.

Now, as Becky pushed onward, panic resumed control. She was growing more and more tired. It wouldn't be long before her body gave up on her.

Keeping going. You're halfway there. Soon, you'll be home free.

Her fingers slid off the wall and swept through empty space. She stumbled forward. Pain punctuated every step. *Corridor number two.* Reaching her hand out in front, she shortened her already minuscule stride and shuffled forward a few centimetres at a time. Just as panic turned to hysteria, the wall came up to meet her.

Becky yelped. Her cry bounced off the wall and the ground, and flew around her head like bats. The echo seemed to go on forever. It started to sound a lot like someone was calling her name: *Becky, Becky, Becky, Becky!* There was a gleefulness to the voice. It was taunting her. She tried to shut it out but then the voice was changing once more. Now it was a soft drip, repeated over and over, just like she had heard before. Water splashing softly against metal.

She was going to lose her mind before she reached the ladder.

"Come on," she gasped, her throat dry as old parchment. "Almost . . . there. . ."

Ignoring the yearning of her body that the splashes of water produced, she staggered on. She had slowed right down, barely moving faster than a child learning to crawl. But she was still moving. A few centimetres forward. A few more. Beneath her fingers, the wall was becoming slick and mossy.

A few more steps. Now, her fingers were slipping in slimy wetness. The dripping sounds were getting louder, and if she were not mistaken, they were coming from somewhere in front of her.

Keep it together! None of this is real. You're almost there.

Cold crept up from the ground. It seeped from the wall and into her fingers. Becky froze. Had she felt something brush past her legs? Something cold and subtle. Like a breeze. She brought her fingers to her nose. There was a smell, damp and musty, like earth after rain. She ran her fingers along her parchment-like lips. She felt moisture.

You have lost your mind.

She shuffled forward. The pain in her ankle was beginning to numb. She didn't know whether this was a good thing or a bad thing. She suspected the latter. *One more step, you can do it!* Her fingers slipped through moss and slime. The wall disappeared. Becky stumbled into black, fathomless space.

She'd made it.

She stood, teetering from side to side, left arm hanging by her side. The sounds of splashing water were louder than ever. There was that tingling sensation again: cold and brisk like a night-time chill.

Except it wasn't night-time.

Turning ninety degrees, Becky stared into the corridor. Her heart, which had become slow and lethargic, began thudding with hope. A few metres down the corridor, there was a thin shaft of vertical light. Illuminated by the light was a steel ladder. Water was dripping from rung to rung and pooling on the floor.

Becky stared at the ladder. Her eyelids drooped. With each step the ladder seemed to move further away. She shook her head and regretted it instantly as pain shot through her skull. She inched closer.

There was something on the ground, lying on the edge of the light. Becky came closer. It was a shoe. It was *her* shoe. Confused, she stared down at her feet. A little light spilled over the toes of her bare right foot.

Had she been hobbling around the whole time with one shoe on, one shoe off? How was her shoe here by the ladder? Her mind swirled like a kaleidoscope. This was where she had been thrown down. Did that mean she'd been lying unconscious by the exit the whole time? Had she imagined the last hours, or had she woken up and wandered off into the darkness before blacking out once more? She stared at the shoe, then at her feet. *The shoe isn't real. The water running down the ladder isn't real.* She didn't like how she was feeling. She didn't like the way her thoughts were no longer making sense.

The ladder.

She inched toward it. Three more steps. Two.

Becky stood before it. She stared up and was blinded by light. Water splashed on her skin, cold and wet. It felt heavenly. She didn't know what was real and what was in her mind.

She didn't care.

Plunging forward, she wrapped her arm around the ladder and brought her lips to the closest rung. She sucked up water, slurping loudly. She held her head back and opened her mouth, letting the water rain in.

She felt like a flower being brought back to life. It was like a dream.

Minutes passed. Becky drank and drank. The ladder felt real. The water running down the back of her throat felt real. More than that. It felt *alive*. Suddenly overcome, Becky felt the urge to cry. She resisted. Her body needed to keep the water inside.

She drank more. Her leg complained bitterly about the weight it was carrying. She perched her right buttock on the ladder and continued to drink, not caring that the water was soaking her skin and her clothes, or that it was beginning to chill her bones.

When she could drink no more, she clung to the ladder and peered up into the light. About three metres above her head, at the top of the ladder, there was a hatch. The hatch door had not been sealed properly, letting light and water seep in.

It was daylight, Becky realised. It was her way out.

She thought about crying for help. Instead, she listened.

No sounds came from above. No voices. No street sounds. No overhead rumbles of a passing car. The only sound was the splash of water hitting metal.

Wherever she was, it was remote, which meant getting out of here was only the beginning of her problems. But Becky was not going to think about that right now. There was a much greater problem facing her; one that she was increasingly unsure she could solve: she needed to get up the ladder.

At least three metres of climbing stood between her and freedom. She could barely stand. Her left arm was broken. Her left foot was a mess.

It's impossible. The voice whispered in her ear. *Come back to the dark. You can sleep and dream.*

Becky shook her head, sending shock waves of pain through her skull. The voice stopped whispering.

"You *can* do this," she said aloud. Now that her throat was lubricated, she sounded almost like her old self. A horribly injured, near death version of her old self, but no less determined for it.

She wrapped her fingers around the outside of the ladder. "Get up you fucking loser. Get up or you're going to fucking die."

Closing her eyes, she pushed her foot against the ground and used the ladder to pull herself up. She was standing. Sort of. All she had to do now was get her foot onto the bottom rung.

That was how she was going to do this. By focusing on one rung at a time. And by hoping that she didn't fall.

Sucking in a deep, painful breath, Becky lifted her left leg and placed her foot on the bottom rung. Careful not to touch her broken arm, she gripped the rung closest to her head with her right hand, exhaled, and pulled up.

Weight crashed down on her ankle. Pain shot through it and up to her jaw, making her teeth smash together. She hauled herself up until both feet were now on the bottom rung. She let her weight shift to the right side of her body and hung there for a second, blinking away white spots and splashes of water.

Becky stared up at the hatch, into the white light. Leaning against the ladder, she reached for the next rung.

"You can do this," she insisted. "You can."

Carefully moving her left foot up to the next rung, Becky clenched her jaw and hauled herself up.

This time, the pain was blinding.

16

ANGER BUBBLED IN the pit of Emily's stomach as she exited Vice Chancellor Eriksson's office and stormed past the PA's desk. By the time she had left the admin building, anger had exploded into full-on fury.

She felt humiliated, belittled. She could still hear Eriksson's words chastising her as she walked through the network of buildings and toward the quad. He had been very clear—Emily was very lucky that Councillor Beaumont was not going to press charges against her for trespassing on private property, even though he was well within his rights.

"And the fact that Bill has sat here and argued your corner while you've accused him of doing Miss Briar harm is a credit to his humility," Vice Chancellor Eriksson had added. He'd paused then, as if he'd been waiting for Emily to apologise to the lecturer, or perhaps even thank him. Emily had done neither. She'd sat in stony silence, trying to make herself invisible.

Eriksson was unhappy about the rumour mill that would now undoubtedly churn out fabricated stories about Bill Creed's involvement in the disappearance of Becky Briar.

"Have you heard the phrase 'mud sticks'?" Eriksson had asked her. "Bill Creed is an excellent educator, who has championed you. Quantock University has an excellent reputation that I will not see tarnished by rumours and fanciful ideas based on wild accusations."

Emily had briefly thought about arguing her case, to reiterate her earlier point that she had made no accusations whatsoever, but had merely reported her findings to Officer Andrews. And weren't they all worrying a little too much about their reputations when a young woman was still missing?

Reaching the quad, Emily pushed past groups of students. Where was she even going? She should return home. Have a hot bath, drink some tea, calm the hell down. Then she should study. Her final exams were drawing nearer and nearer.

Becky is still missing.

Something hadn't felt wrong in the Vice Chancellor's office. Why had the three men felt it necessary to band together like that? Wouldn't a stern warning from the Vice Chancellor alone be enough to chastise a wayward student? The meeting felt deliberate, as if the men had discussed the most effective way to put an end to Emily's interference. What were they so worried about? Surely they weren't intimidated by her?

Emily walked on a few steps before coming to a halt. Not one of those men—not even Bill Creed—had expressed any deep concern about Becky's whereabouts. Even if she had run away, didn't they care about the wellbeing of a vulnerable young woman? One known to all three of them.

Anger still bubbling away, Emily turned and marched out of the quad. Ideas and notions flew through her mind. The more she thought about it, the more she felt something was wrong. The way the men had stood so deliberately apart, forming a wall around her. The nervous glances Bill Creed had fired in Vice Chancellor Eriksson's direction. The way Eriksson's left eye had twitched at the mention of drug dealers.

And what was all that about Officer Andrews' report? She wondered what the policeman would have to say about the little meeting she'd just endured. And, as a matter of a fact, she had a few questions for Officer Andrews about how that meeting could have been orchestrated in the first place.

Emily called the police station, asked for Andrews, and was put on hold. While she waited to be connected, she made her way to the main gates. Turning a corner, she walked straight into a group of girls.

Her heart leapt as she came face to face with Damien's girlfriend, Tamara.

Tamara's eyes grew wide and piercing. Before Emily could react, Tamara threw a hand up in the air and brought it down hard on Emily's left cheek.

Emily saw brilliant white. Stinging pain erupted across her face. Her phone flew from her fingers and clattered on the ground.

"Fucking bitch!" Tamara hissed. "Damien's been arrested. I hope you're happy!"

Emily clutched her face, which was now a deep shade of red and smarting like hell.

A large vein pulsated at the centre of Tamara's forehead. "I told you to mind your own business but look what you've done. You fucking snitch! He could go to prison!"

Emily said nothing. Part of her wanted to retaliate. To hit the girl square in the mouth. Part of her wanted to grab her phone and run. Instead, she slowly rubbed her cheek, not daring to take her eyes off Tamara as the girl raged on.

"What? Because you're some Miss Goody Two-Shoes virgin you think you can go around snitching on people, ruining their lives because you're so much better than them? You stupid whore!"

Before Emily could duck, Tamara spat in her face. A thick globule of saliva hit Emily's temple and ran over her fingers.

"I hope that bitch Becky is never found," Tamara said, her face dangerously close to Emily's. "I hope she's dead somewhere. You better watch your step. You better make sure you don't end up the same."

With those parting words, Tamara nodded to her friends, shot Emily a final, warning glance, and marched away. The other girls followed.

Emily remained quite still, her hand clutched to her cheek. No one else had witnessed the provocation. If she reported it, it would be her word against Tamara and her followers.

A voice, distant and tinny, caught her attention.

Scooping her phone up from the ground, she pressed it to her ear.

"Emily? Are you there? Hello? Are you all right?"

"I'm here," she said. Her voice cracked. "I'm fine."

"You don't sound fine," Officer Andrews said. "What was all that ruckus?"

"Nothing." She shut her eyes. She could feel her cheek pulsating, the skin tightening as the tissue swelled. "Have you found Becky?"

Officer Andrews hesitated. "Not yet. But-"

"I've just had a very interesting meeting," Emily said.

The pain in her face radiated upward, triggering the beginnings of a headache. An angry tear shot from her eye.

"Oh?"

"Yes, with Vice Chancellor Eriksson, Bill Creed, and Councillor Beaumont, as a matter of fact. They all decided to get together and give me a good telling off."

The line was quiet.

"Emily, I'm sorry," Officer Andrews said. "That's not... That wasn't very fair of them."

"Oh, I don't know. They have their integrity to uphold. They don't need some silly little girl like me getting in their way."

"I feel responsible. I encouraged you to ask questions. Obviously, I didn't mean you should go trespassing on Councillor Beaumont's property but-"

"Forget it. It's water under the bridge," Emily was on the move again, heading to the campus gates. She nodded at the security guard sitting in his booth. The gates swung open. "Besides, I learned something new. On Monday night, Becky left the Beaumont's in a taxi. If you had the taxi company's number, you could find out where they really took her."

"I'm one step ahead of you," Officer Andrews said.

"Oh?"

As Emily passed through the gates, the security guard stared at her swelling cheek. She turned away, quickening her step.

Officer Andrews cleared his throat. "The taxi company's records show that Becky requested to be taken to the train station. The driver confirmed he dropped her off at approximately 9 PM."

"But how do you know that she actually got on a train?"

"Because I'm a police officer. Believe it or not, I'm pretty good at my job. Besides, she was caught on CCTV buying a ticket."

Stunned, Emily stopped in the middle of the street.

"Emily, I'm afraid it looks like Becky has decided to take off. As far as I can tell, she owed money to a lot of people, she was more than likely having issues with drugs, and she had certainly failed her degree."

"Stop talking about her in the past tense. She's not dead."

"I'm sorry. But I should tell you that based on the evidence we've gathered, it's obvious what's happened. Hopefully, she'll show up at some point soon, when she's ready. But for now, I'm afraid there's nothing else we can do."

"Did the CCTV show her getting onto the train? How about interviewing the staff? Or questioning Damien Harris—you do still have him in custody, don't you?"

There was a pause before Officer Andrews spoke again. "I'm sorry, Emily, but unless crucial evidence turns up, something untoward…then it's out of our hands. I've filed my report. You can try and follow it up with Missing Persons, but they're a charity not the police; they'll be able to put together a social media campaign, posters…It's down to the Briar family if they want to continue searching for her."

"So that's it? You're dropping the case?"

"There's no case to drop." Officer Andrews apologised again. "Hopefully Becky will get in touch with somebody when she's ready. In the meantime, the best thing you can do is get on with things. You have exams coming up, I hear. Harassing important figures such as Councillor Beaumont isn't going to do you or anyone else any favours."

Too angry to speak, Emily reached the bus stop and sat down.

"Well, if that's all…" Officer Andrews mumbled.

"What if something has happened to her?" Emily said at last. "What if she's hurt or…worse?"

But Officer Andrews had already hung up.

Emily slumped down on the bus shelter bench. A lone woman sat on the other end, trying not to stare at Emily's swollen face. Had she been wrong all this time? Her mind circled the events of the last few days, over and over, trying to find something she'd missed. She returned to the meeting in Vice Chancellor Eriksson's office.

Further down the road, a bus turned the corner. More people appeared at the bus stop. Why was she so insistent that something terrible had happened to Becky? Why couldn't she believe the facts just like everyone else?

The bus pulled in. Feeling miserable, Emily stood up. She touched her face and immediately regretted it. Becky had been missing for at least four days. The police were about to drop the investigation. Everyone had turned their backs.

Her heart swelling, Emily boarded the bus and planted herself in a window seat, hiding her bruised cheek from the other passengers. It felt a lot like time had run out.

17

BECKY

SOMEHOW, SHE HAD almost made it to the top. The muscles in her arm begged for rest. Her left leg was all but useless. Pain had almost toppled her twice. Once, she had slipped in water and come dangerously close to falling. Another time, she had almost given up and let the darkness take her.

Now, with just a few more rungs to go, with light pouring over her face, Becky felt a last desperate rush of determination. If she gave up now, she would be a laughing stock in the afterlife. If there even was an afterlife.

Clamping her jaw shut, she hauled herself up to the next rung. She waited a full minute and hauled herself up to the next.

The hatch was within arm's reach. The problem was that she only had one working arm.

But she had made it this far. By some miracle, she had been able to climb the ladder. She could not give up now. She would not allow herself to be defeated when freedom was just half a metre away.

Leaning her full weight against the ladder, she reached up and brushed her fingers against the hatch door. It was cold and wet. The locking mechanism was different to that of the main door. This one consisted of a handle that, when turned, would open the hatch outward.

Becky's fingers grazed the tip of the handle, moving to the edge of the hatch where light streamed in. What if none of this was real? What if she was still down there somewhere, lying face down in the dark, the last fragments of her life crumbling to dust. The light felt real. She ran her fingertips along the gap. A breeze brushed over her hand. And there were sounds. Leaves rustling on trees. A bird singing somewhere high above.

It had to be real.

But she had to move now. Soon, she would have no strength left at all, and there would be nothing to stop her from tumbling back into darkness.

Pressing her body into the ladder and pushing down on her good foot, Becky wrapped her fingers around the handle. She pulled.

Nothing happened.

She pulled again. This time, she heard a dull grate of metal. Rust fell, sprinkling her head.

"Come on!" she hissed through clenched teeth.

She pulled again, drawing on her remaining strength. Metal screeched. Large chunks of rust rained down.

The handle turned ninety degrees. And came away in Becky's hand.

She could feel herself tipping backward, the weight of the handle pulling her away from the ladder.

Instinctively, she released her grip. Her hand shot forward and gripped a rung. There was a long, terrible silence. Below her, the handle hit the floor with a deafening clatter.

Becky clung to the ladder, breathing hard and fast.

She was going to die. There was nothing she could do about it. Her last chance was used up.

Tears came, and with them, a terror so absolute it consumed her entire being.

She was going to die.

Alone. In the dark.

It would be a horrible, drawn out death.

Trembling uncontrollably, Becky opened her mouth and let out a strangled, horrified scream.

18

CHARLOTTE WAS UPSTAIRS when Emily arrived home, sitting on her bedroom floor as she attempted to take apart a chest of drawers. An open suitcase lay on the bed, half filled with clothes. Emily tried to creep past the open door, not wanting conversation but to hide away in her room with the curtains closed.

"Jesus, what happened to your face?!"

Charlotte leapt up, staring at Emily's cheek.

Emily heaved her shoulders.

"Damien Harris' girlfriend happened to my face," she said. She moved into the room and, negotiating the piles of Charlotte's belongings on the floor, checked her reflection in the dresser mirror. The left side of her face was red and puffy. There was still a faint outline of fingers on her skin. Tamara certainly knew how to leave her mark.

"She hit you?" Charlotte said, mouth agape. "Have you called the police?"

Emily had thought about it but already changed her mind. If the police weren't interested in the disappearance of Becky Briar, were they really going to do anything about some upstart of a first-year student?

Emily found a corner on the bed and sat down.

"Let me guess—this was revenge for getting Damien

arrested." Charlotte picked up the screwdriver again.

"How do you know about that?"

"Word travels fast."

It certainly did. Emily glanced around the room. "What is all this? You're leaving already?"

Charlotte nodded, her face turning red as she struggled to loosen a screw on the chest of drawers. "Tomorrow. Us history undergrads had our finals last week. You know this. I told you like a hundred times."

"Sorry. I've been distracted."

"Still no word on Becky?"

Emily filled her in on the events of the last twenty-four hours: her encounter with Damien Harris, Beaumont House; the meeting with Vice Chancellor Eriksson, Councillor Beaumont, and Bill Creed; the CCTV footage showing Becky at the train station.

Charlotte was quiet for a long time, sadness tinging her eyes. "So, she really did run away. What do we do with her things?"

Giving up on the stuck screw, she passed the screwdriver to Emily and cleared a space for her on the floor.

"I'll talk to her mother and see if she wants me to pack them up."

"I'm sorry I won't be around to help, Em. I feel bad leaving in the middle of it all but I've already booked the removal people. They'll be here at two tomorrow afternoon."

"Don't worry about it." The screw wouldn't budge. Emily leaned into it, clenching her teeth.

"How about you? When are you leaving?"

The screw turned a few millimetres. "As soon as the exams are done."

"So, you've decided what you're doing?"

Emily grunted. The screw turned and loosened.

"I'll decide once the exams are over," she said. It was the closest to a decision she could make right now. "Here."

Charlotte stared at the screw in her palm then added it to the others. Without warning, she threw her arms around Emily's shoulders and pulled her in.

"It's been great living with you," she said. "You've been my voice of reason. I'm going to miss that."

Emily felt a little of the tension in her shoulders fade. She folded into Charlotte's embrace.

"Now, go and get some ice. Before you end up looking like the Elephant Man."

Emily mustered a smile. It hurt like hell. "I'll miss you too."

Leaving the room, she went to head downstairs for a bag of frozen peas. Instead, she found herself pushing open Becky's bedroom door.

Sunlight poured in. Motes of dust danced in the beams. The air was stale. Emily crossed the room and opened the window. She stood for a while, her eyes roaming the mess of Becky's belongings. A thought returned to press on her conscience: What if everybody was wrong?

She went to the wardrobe. Becky's clothes still hung from hangers and filled the upper shelves. Her suitcases sat beneath her bed, collecting dust. The only obvious missing element was her laptop. Perhaps she had sold it. If she was in as much debt as Officer Andrews suggested it was possible Becky had sold all her valuables.

Emily cast another glance across the room. Was it worth having one last look? Officer Andrews had already conducted a search but that was before they'd learned about Becky's activities. Perhaps there was something here the police officer had missed.

"Or perhaps you're beating a dead horse," Emily muttered.

She began with the bedside drawers. Finding nothing she pulled out the suitcases from beneath the bed. Next, she moved over to the dressing table. Various items of makeup sat on top, along with the jewellery box. There were no family pictures, Emily noted. In fact, looking around the room, there were no photographs of Becky's family anywhere

Emily stared at the jewellery box. It was old and battered, the silk exterior frayed at the corners. She flipped it open. The tiny ballerina leapt up. Music began to play. A few pairs of cheap earrings sat inside next to a couple of plastic bracelets. Emily picked up one of the bracelets, which was made up of black beads. On each bead was a tiny white skull. It was typical Becky, she thought. Or was it? She didn't know Becky at all. Not like she had thought.

Picking up the receipts Officer Andrews had found, Emily unfolded the top one. It was for a sale of £30; a transaction made at an establishment known as Rockin' Roy's Pawn Shop.

A guilty weight sat on Emily's shoulders. Why hadn't Becky said anything? Why hadn't she reached out and asked for help? Emily was not wealthy. Far from it. In fact, there were times growing up when birthday presents were little more than a second-hand toy from one of the charity shops over in Penzance. But what she lacked in funds, she made up for in resourcefulness. She could have helped Becky to find a way out of this mess.

She shuffled the receipts. There were seven in total, some for a few pounds, others for a few hundred, all sharing the same date: 5th June. None stated the items pawned.

Emily eyed the other objects on the dressing table. The feeling that she was missing something pulled at her chest. She went over the events of the last few days again, unpicking them, playing and replaying scenes in her mind. No matter which path she took, each one returned her to the same place: Vice Chancellor Eriksson's office. Her unconscious was trying to tell her something. But what?

Emily's heart beat a little faster. She turned to face the room.

What had she missed?

She searched the room again. Ten minutes later, Emily found it. But what she found left her even more confused.

Charlotte had moved downstairs to the kitchen. She yelped as Emily burst in, waving a notebook in the air.

"That boy who ended up in the hospital, what was his name?"

"I have no idea what you're talking about."

"The boy Damien Harris attacked last year."

Charlotte squinted. "Michael Nowak. But what has this got to do with-"

Emily thrust the notebook in front of Charlotte's face. On the page, scrawled in Becky's spidery handwriting, was: *Michael Nowak, 2 PM, 8th June.* An address was scrawled underneath.

"Look at the date," Emily said. "That's less than two weeks ago. What was Becky doing meeting with Michael Nowak?"

"Who knows what Becky's been up to? Clearly, nothing good." Charlotte stared at Emily, concern lining her face. "What are you thinking?"

Emily stabbed the notebook with her index finger. "What if this Michael Nowak knows something? What if it's something to do with why Becky's run away?"

"I thought we'd established that. She ran away because she owes a ton of money to a known drug dealer."

"A known drug dealer who beat Michael Nowak to a pulp..."

"Emily, the police have already filed the report. Becky's gone," Charlotte said, suddenly exasperated. "Why are you insisting on pushing this when you've got other things to worry about? Like your finals, for example. Or your future career."

Emily heaved her shoulders. "What if we're all wrong? No one actually saw Becky get on a train. Everyone's given up. If I give up, then she has no one."

"Becky didn't care about you. She didn't care about either of us. She made a mess of her life and she's run off, leaving the rest of us to tidy up after her. Speaking to Michael Nowak isn't going to change that."

Becky's untidy handwriting leapt up from the page.

Charlotte was right, Emily thought. But she had to try. Even if it was to rid herself of the dread that was now gnawing away at her like a dog on an old bone.

19

SATURDAY

MICHAEL NOWAK LIVED fifty minutes north-east, in the city of Bristol. Emily had not wanted to come all this way but he had insisted on discussing the matter in person. Now, she sat in the living room of a large town house, the half-closed curtains letting in little light, while Michael sat in the chair opposite, twisting his fingers in knots.

He was a gaunt young man, pale and haunted, with a mess of dark hair, sharp cheekbones, and wide, pale eyes, which regarded Emily with a nervous distrust.

She had arrived only a few minutes ago, and had been welcomed in by Michael's mother, a middle-aged woman with a kind face who seemed delighted her son was receiving a visitor. She had set about making coffee and brought in a tray with chocolate cookies, all the while flashing Emily enthused looks. When she eventually left them alone, Emily and Michael Nowak stared awkwardly at each other as silence draped the room.

"So, you want to know about Damien Harris," Michael said at last, in a hushed voice. "About what he did to me."

Emily leaned forward a little and showed him Becky's notebook. "As I explained last night, my friend Becky is missing. She-"

"I thought you said she'd run away."

"Yes, but—I think she's in trouble. I'm trying to find out what kind of trouble. Your name was-"

"Why?"

"Pardon me?"

"Why are you trying to find out?"

Emily stared at him, the notebook still extended in her hand. "Because if she's in trouble, I want to help."

"Maybe she doesn't want your help," Michael said. He shifted slightly, his face tightening as if the movement had caused him pain. "Maybe she just wants to be left alone."

"It's possible, I suppose. But does that mean I shouldn't try?"

"What if the trouble is of her own doing?"

"What if it is? People make mistakes. Sometimes they need help with making things right."

Emily dropped the notebook on her lap. Silence filled the space between them once more.

Michael reached for his coffee. His fingers trembled.

"I'm sorry if I seem rude," he said. "But I hadn't heard Damien Harris' name in almost a year. Now you're the second person to ask about him. He's not someone I want to remember."

"I didn't come here to cause you further pain," Emily said. She glanced down at the notebook. "You said I was the second person. Becky was the first?"

Michael nodded. "She showed up a couple of weeks ago. I vaguely remembered her face from university. She wanted to know about Damien, about what he did to me. About the fact no charges were brought against him."

Emily had been wondering that herself. "I heard Damien

put you in the hospital. You must have been badly hurt."

"That's one way of putting it. He broke my arm in two places, fractured my skull, crushed my hand...I was a music student. I used to play the piano."

He sat for a moment, staring into space at a life that might have been if Damien Harris hadn't destroyed it.

Suddenly, Emily felt guilty for coming here.

"Michael, I-"

"Please. I'm so sick of everyone's pity. You came here to ask questions about your friend Becky. So, ask."

He seemed to fold into himself, sitting limply like an old man.

Feeling wretched, Emily drew in a breath. "Why was Becky asking about Damien?"

Michael shrugged a shoulder. "Because he's a dangerous fucking bastard and she wanted dirt on him. Something she could use to protect herself. That's my guess, anyway."

"And you gave her something she could use?"

"Maybe."

"What does that mean?"

"It means she asked questions and I answered them. Same as we're doing now. Only, she was better at asking the right questions."

He stared at her with a raised eyebrow but said nothing more.

Emily took a second to refocus. "Fine. Why did Damien Harris attack you?"

"Because he's a psychopath." Michael smiled. "There I was, walking along to my next class, my head in the clouds as usual. I turned the corner and...bam, I walked straight into Damien and his girlfriend. Me being me, I mumbled an apology and moved on. I knew who Damien was—

someone you never wanted to look in the eye—so I tried to get out of there as fast as I could. But Damien had different ideas.

"He grabbed me as I walked away, dragged me back to his girlfriend, demanded I apologise properly." The smile had left Michael's lips. He clasped his hands together and began massaging his fingers. "Jesus, it was like being back at school. I honestly thought university would be different. That I'd be surrounded by young adults with mature minds. That idiots like Damien Harris got crappy jobs and drinking problems, and knocked around their girlfriends."

"What happened next?"

"I apologised in front of a packed audience. God, it was embarrassing. Everyone staring. No one doing a damn thing to help. I apologised, but that didn't seem good enough for Damien. He was about to take it outside when his girlfriend intervened. She told him enough was enough, to let me go. He did, reluctantly, but not without telling me to watch my back. Like a coward, I nodded and apologised again. But as I walked away, something came over me.

"I suppose it was the realisation that university was no better than school. That wherever you go, there will always be people like Damien Harris; angry at the world, thinking everyone owes them a favour, and determined to take out their frustrations on poor unsuspecting bastards like me. It pissed me off. So, as I was leaving, I gave him the middle finger." His eyes lit up at the memory. "I felt very daring at the time. Like I was saying a big *fuck you* to everyone who had ever pushed me around."

Emily leaned forward, already knowing how this story ended. "And Damien attacked you?"

"Not right away. I ran for it, expecting to be tackled to

the ground. I assumed his girlfriend had stopped him. But he was just biding his time. He waited a couple of days until I thought I was safe. He tracked me down one evening. I'd had a few drinks in the student bar; not enough to get drunk but enough to let my guard down. Damien followed me. He waited until I was alone, then he jumped me.

"I don't remember much after that. I recall him straddling me. I remember his words. He said: 'No one gives me the middle finger without getting one back.' He snapped my fingers with his bare hands. The rest is just images thankfully. Blurs. I woke up in hospital. There were police, waiting to question me, wanting me to identify my attacker. I gave them that asshole's name and hoped that he'd rot in prison."

Emily wrinkled her forehead and stared at Becky's notebook. "I don't understand—Damien Harris wasn't charged."

"That's not strictly true," Michael said. "The police arrested him. He was interrogated. DNA samples were taken. The police were confident he was going to go down for assault."

"So, what happened?"

"I refused to press charges."

Emily was aghast. "Why would you do that? He beat you to a pulp. He destroyed your career before it had even begun."

Across the table, Michael folded his arms over his chest. He was quiet for a long while, the frown on his brow burrowing deeper with each passing second.

"While I was convalescing in hospital, I was visited by Damien Harris' father. He begged me not to press charges against his son. He said that Damien was a very troubled young man who needed help. Prison would only set him down a dark road. He blamed himself for a lot of his son's behaviour. He and Damien's mother were divorced, you see. He'd walked out on the family when Damien was eleven."

"That doesn't excuse what his son did to you," Emily said, thinking of her own absent father; the difference being she had never met hers. "And it doesn't explain why you dropped the charges."

"Damien's father offered me money. A lot of money. He offered to pay for private medical treatment. I accepted his offer, not because I felt sorry for him or for Damien, but because I thought it was the only way I could salvage my career. Oh, I'm sure treatment on the National Health Service would have got me on my feet again. But at the time, I was convinced the only way I could save my hand was by getting the very best treatment. It was something I couldn't afford. My family are far from rich. So, I took a chance. Damien's father drew up a contract. I was sworn to secrecy. And I kept my secret until the day your friend showed up."

Emily leaned back, a maelstrom of conflicting emotions clashing in her head.

"Did he keep his word?" she asked.

Michael raised his hand and fanned out his fingers. "The surgeon set them perfectly. Unfortunately, the arthritis that followed ensured the most I could play was *Chopsticks*. But by then it was too late. I'd been paid thousands of pounds. I'd signed a contract promising my silence."

"And why break that contract now? What was Becky doing here?"

"She wanted to know the same thing you're asking

yourself now."

Emily caught her breath. "Who is Damien's father?"

Michael smiled and clasped his trembling hands together. "You know what people love? People love a good scandal. It doesn't matter whether the facts are substantiated or not. Once the rumour mill gets going, it's very, very difficult to stop. Reputations are destroyed. Lives are ruined. Even if those rumours prove to be unfounded."

"What are you saying?" Emily's mind raced. Becky had learned of Michael's agreement with Damien's father. Then she had discovered his identity. What had she done with that information? Emily looked up. Suddenly, she knew.

Across the room, Michael's lips parted into a cruel grin. "I smell blackmail."

20

EMILY WAITED UNTIL she was off the train to call Charlotte. It was just past midday and the town centre was busy with shoppers. Bored teenagers hung out in the town square, idling on benches and riding skateboards. Above them, the sky was liquid blue.

"Emily, where are you? I'm leaving in two hours. You *said* you'd be here."

Breaking into a sweat, Emily pulled off her jacket. "I know. I'm sorry. I'm on my way back right now."

A loud crash rang out in Emily's ear, followed by a round of expletives.

"Great, I'll leave all the heavy lifting for you," Charlotte said. Suspicion filled her voice. "Where have you been? Did you go and see Michael Nowak?"

Leaving the square, Emily headed down a cobbled street, past a vegan cafe and an antique shop. "Yes, I did."

"Jesus, Em. What are you doing? You should be here studying."

"I thought I was supposed to be lifting boxes."

"You know what I mean." Charlotte paused. "What was he like?"

"Bitter. Understandably so, given the circumstances."

"And what *are* the circumstances?"

Emily glanced over her shoulder at a couple walking behind, their hands linked and their arms swinging. "I'll tell you about it when I get home."

"And when will that be?"

"Thirty minutes. I need to do something first. I promise I won't be long."

"Right."

Emily reached the end of the street. She mumbled an apology, promised to be home soon, and hung up. She stood still, contemplating her next move.

The campus was a ten-minute walk to her left. It being Saturday, the place would be a ghost town. The police station was three streets away to her right. She could deliver the information she'd learned from Michael Nowak to Officer Andrews, or to one of his colleagues. But would they act upon it? As far as they were concerned, Becky Briar was no longer at risk. She was an adult with a legal entitlement to disappear. What would they do with this new information? It certainly didn't point to Becky's whereabouts, and even if it did, the information was only hearsay. Michael Nowak would never come forward.

"Screw it," Emily muttered under her breath.

She turned and headed toward the campus.

21

THE CAMPUS WAS almost empty. Only a handful of students milled about, making their way to the library or to the main gates. Emily kept her head down and her jaw clamped shut as she strode past the Education department. Reaching the Administration block, she came to a halt. She watched the entrance for a full minute and wondered what the hell she was doing here. *Putting your career at risk, that's what.*

Sucking in a calming breath, she made her way inside.

The reception desk was empty. She could hear the hum of electricity, the *blop* of rising bubbles in the water cooler. She thought about calling out but changed her mind. She could take a quick look. In and out in two minutes before anyone could notice.

Taking one last cursory glance over her shoulder, Emily hurried past the reception desk and into a dimly lit corridor.

Doors lay on both sides. The one she wanted lay at the end. Her breaths coming loud and fast, she pressed her ear to the wood and listened. Silence. She tried the handle. The door popped open. Emily stepped inside Vice Chancellor Eriksson's office.

Her heart was already pounding inside her chest but now it drummed even louder.

Leaving the door open, she reached the centre of the room and turned a full circle. She glanced at the empty armchair in which Bill Creed had sat, then at the space in front of the window. Memories of yesterday's meeting played in her mind, igniting sparks of anger.

She turned her attention to Vice Chancellor Eriksson's large mahogany desk. It was busy but neatly arranged. A wall of bookshelves stood behind it, filled with encyclopaedias, almanacs, yearbooks, and photographs. More framed pictures hung on the wall to the right—black and white images of the university; portraits of previous Vice Chancellors. A coat stand stood in the far corner, thankfully empty.

Emily headed straight to the bookshelves and examined the photographs. One was of Eriksson shaking hands with the town mayor; another of him meeting the previous prime minister.

There was just one photograph of his family. It had been taken in a leafy garden. Eriksson was dressed in smart casual wear—he hadn't struck Emily as a man who wore jeans—and he stared at the camera with his head tipped slightly back, his lips flat and still.

Beside him, his hand placed purposefully on her shoulder, was a woman of similar age, with sharp features and black, wiry hair. His wife, Emily presumed. Unlike her husband, Mrs Eriksson smiled widely at the camera, although her smile did not reach her eyes, Emily noted.

To the right of Mrs Eriksson was a thin girl who looked much younger than she was dressed. Her clothes were expensive looking, her jewellery definitely not costume. Like her father—Emily could see the resemblance straight away—the girl stared at the camera in defiance.

Emily picked up the photograph. *Happy families*, she thought. She returned her attention to the Vice Chancellor's desk. Now faced with the open door, she found her eyes drawn to the corridor beyond. Her chest tightened. *Let's get this over with.*

She began with the filing tray sat on top of the desk. A quick shuffle through the papers revealed work-related documents, nothing that was relevant. A small framed photograph of a black and white border collie sat beside the telephone, a great, slathering tongue lolling from its mouth. Emily's eyes moved down to the drawers.

There were three in total. The first contained headed university notepaper and several foil strips of antihistamines. The middle drawer contained yet more documents, plus a thick, black diary. Emily quickly leafed through the pages. All the appointments inside were work-related: board meetings, patron meetings, student and lecturer appointments, business and charity dinners. Everything looked above board.

Emily tried the final drawer. At first, she thought it was locked. Then, giving it a rough tug, the drawer opened. Peering in, she raised an eyebrow. So, she thought, even Vice Chancellors kept a junk drawer.

She made fast work of searching through its contents, pushing past loose stationery, paper clips, boxes of staplers, packets of tissues, a couple of empty chocolate bar wrappers. Her fingernails caught on something at the bottom. She fished it out.

A rush of adrenaline pulsed through Emily's veins. In her hand, she held an unframed photograph. It had been taken many summers ago. In it, a younger Vice Chancellor Eriksson wore a navy polo shirt and khaki shorts. He was down on one knee and smiling at the camera. It was a genuine smile, Emily thought.

Eriksson was not the only person in the photograph. Standing next to him, leaning into the crook of his arm, was a young boy about six years old. He was thin-framed, with a mop of blonde hair that fell across his brow. Soft brown eyes peeked out from beneath, regarding the camera with an expression somewhere between curiosity and wariness.

Emily glanced up from the picture and stared at the framed photograph on the shelf. Two different families from two different times: one on display for the world to see, the other dumped at the bottom of a junk drawer like a dirty secret.

She felt a sudden pity for Damien Harris. Is this what could happen when your father ran out on you? She'd never known her own father. Her mother had said he'd left the day he'd found out she was pregnant. Emily didn't even know his name, or whether he was alive or dead. "What's the point of knowing," her mother had told her each time she'd asked, "when he'd rather you didn't exist?" Eventually, Emily decided she couldn't really miss someone she'd never met, and stopped asking about him.

But for Damien, his father had been there for the first part of his life, and judging by the photograph, there had been a strong bond between father and son. Then Eriksson had disappeared. What kind of emotional damage had that inflicted on the boy? Had his father's departure been the catalyst for a life fuelled by anger and bitterness, a desire to do wrong?

Emily stared into young Damien Harris' eyes. There was only innocence there. What a dreadful shame.

A smell reached Emily's nose.

Coffee, rich and aromatic.

Vice Chancellor Eriksson stood in the doorway, a steaming polystyrene cup in one hand, his jaw slackening like marshmallow.

Emily stopped breathing. The two were frozen, staring at each other.

Eriksson was the first to speak. "Give me one good reason why I shouldn't call the police immediately and have you arrested for breaking and entering."

He remained in the doorway, his eyes flitting between Emily's face and the photograph in her hand.

"The door was open," Emily said. Her throat had dried up, making her voice small and thin. "I didn't break anything."

Eriksson made no move to enter the room. He stood, blocking the only exit. Emily's eyes flitted to the window and back to the Vice Chancellor.

"I told you to leave things alone." Now Eriksson did enter the room, closing the door behind him. "I told you to concentrate on your exams."

The desk was all that stood between them. Eriksson set down his coffee. He held out his hand, nodding at the photograph.

Emily gave it to him and watched as he regarded it for a moment. His face softened. Tenderness filled his eyes. Then it was gone. Wrapping his fingers around the photograph, he crushed it into a ball.

"What do you think you're doing, Emily?" he said.

Emily was silent, watching his every move.

"Are you hoping to continue where that malicious bitch left off?" His eyes flashed dangerously.

Emily took a small step back. "No. That's—I'm not that

132

kind of person. I'm just trying to find out the truth."

Vice Chancellor Eriksson laughed. The photograph was still in his clenched fist.

"The truth? About what exactly? About what a terrible father I am? About how a guilty conscience can lead you to make all kinds of questionable decisions? Is that it? Or would you like to know the truth about your so-called friend, Rebecca Briar? A devious, manipulative little slut who played my son for a fool. Who then attempted to blackmail me when her actions came back to bite her. That's who your friend was, Emily. A liar and a crook; someone whose interests lay with her own personal gain. You think someone like that is worth saving? You think she would care that you're going to such lengths as breaking the law in your quest to help her? I can guarantee with utmost certainty that your name is already a whisper on the wind. Noise. Why risk a promising career for someone who has already forgotten about you?"

Emily glanced down at the desk. A silver letter opener with a sharp blade lay in the filing tray.

"Becky's not like that," she said. "She's in trouble. She needs help. Your son has seen to that."

"My son is an idiot, who is now in police custody thanks to your efforts."

"Nothing to do with the fact he sells drugs to students on campus. Or the fact he has a temper he can't control. But I hear you already know about that."

Anger flashed in Eriksson's eyes. Emily flinched, shocked at the words spilling from her mouth. This was the Vice Chancellor she was speaking to—a man who could take everything she'd worked for and crush it like the photograph still clamped in his fist.

Eriksson glared at her. For a long time, he said nothing. Outside, a brightly coloured jay fluttered down to roost on the hedge. Eriksson crossed the room and stared at it.

"Tell me Emily, what do you think you know?"

Open space stood between Emily and the door. It would be easy to run. But her curiosity was piqued.

"I know Becky found out you were Damien's father," she said. "And that you paid off the boy he almost beat to death."

"Michael Nowak," Eriksson spat. "That little prick is in serious trouble. Once, I've tidied up this mess, he can expect a visit from my lawyer."

"To say what? How dare he tell someone about how you manipulated him when he was at his most vulnerable?"

"He signed a contract."

"He was scared he would never play piano again. You intimidated him."

Eriksson glared at her, his pupils large and round like two black holes.

"You've spoken to him, haven't you?" he said. "Just like that bitch. Once she'd learned about our agreement, she thought she could play me just like she played my son. She came here last week, demanding money. Boasting that she could have my son and I arrested with a snap of her fingers unless I gave her ten grand. That, she said, was the cost of her silence."

"And you paid it?"

"I had no choice. My relationship with Damien was frayed at best. He'd never forgiven me for walking out on him and his mother, for starting a new life and a new family. I tried to fit him in as much as I could—weekends, birthdays—but he failed to understand the responsibilities that my work brought, or how much of my time it devoured. When he enrolled here as an undergraduate, I was shocked. I'd thought he'd wanted nothing more to do with me. Foolishly, I hoped he perhaps wanted to reconcile our relationship.

"When I discovered his *activities* on campus, I was furious. I threatened to have him removed immediately. He told me he would go to the trustees and reveal his identity. He would tell them that I'd known exactly what he was doing. Reluctantly, we came to an arrangement—his discretion in return for mine. It was an uneasy agreement, but it worked. Michael Nowak was a bump in the road but one that I smoothed over.

"Then came Rebecca Briar, threatening to ruin everything. She knew Damien was my son, that I'd been allowing him to conduct his business. But she told me the money was to help her make a fresh start, that she was leaving town and had no intention of returning. Ten thousand was a drop in the ocean if it meant I'd never see her again."

"What about Monday night?" Emily said. "Damien drove her out to Beaumont House. Why?"

Vice Chancellor Eriksson laughed. "Do you really think someone as calculating and opportunistic as Rebecca Briar would stop at blackmailing me?"

"You mean, she. . .?"

"The world of politics is a savage arena, Emily. Difficult decisions must be made if one wants to rise up and lead. I suspect your friend discovered one of those difficult decisions while snooping around Beaumont House. That evening, she came to collect one last time, promising to return the money she owed Damien before leaving for good."

Piece by piece, the events were assembling themselves in Emily's head, but she was still having trouble believing that Becky was capable of such underhand and malicious actions, no matter how much the evidence spoke for itself.

"You and Councillor Beaumont knew of each other's…dealings with Becky?"

"A week before her disappearance, I received a panicked phone call from Councillor Beaumont," Eriksson said. "He was terrified his reputation would be in ruins if his indiscretions were made public."

"And what were those indiscretions?"

"It's not my business to ask. What you need to understand, Emily, is people like Councillor Beaumont and I, people who are placed in positions of power and respect, we must always look out for one another because there will always be those who want to do us harm."

"Someone like Becky Briar."

"Or perhaps, someone like you."

Vice Chancellor Eriksson moved quickly, planting himself between Emily and the door.

Emily's gaze shot to the letter opener on the desk.

Eriksson stepped toward her. "Tell me, Emily, what do you intend to do with the information you've learned?"

Emily pressed herself against the desk. Her fingers fumbled for the letter opener.

"Nothing," she whispered. "Just tell me what happened to Becky. Tell me where she is and I promise I won't say anything."

Eriksson smiled. "And what if I can't do that?"

Her fingertips glanced against the filing tray. "Please. If she's hurt, she'll need help. Or if she's. . ."

"Or if she's what? Dead?" The Vice Chancellor laughed.

"Is that your theory? That Councillor Beaumont and I conspired together to commit murder? To silence our blackmailer for good? What an overactive imagination you have, Emily. Perhaps you should forgo a career in teaching for one in private detection!" He moved closer. "You're a smart girl—think about it logically. Do you honestly believe the councillor and I would put our careers and reputations at further risk by committing murder?"

Palming the letter opener, Emily dropped her hand to her side.

"Perhaps you had someone do it for you," she said. *Someone like your son.* The realisation that Becky could be dead hit her square in the stomach, knocking the breath from her lungs. She stepped back. The bookshelf pressed into her spine.

The Vice Chancellor leaned over the desk. Emily's fingers tightened around the letter opener.

"You want to know the truth?" he said. "I have no idea where Rebecca is. Councillor Beaumont was not lying. She came to his house that night asking for money. What he omitted to mention was exactly how much, and what she was prepared to do if he didn't give it to her. He also excluded the fact that he wrote her a cheque. But he told the truth—his wife called a cab and Becky left in it. The Beaumonts haven't seen her since."

Emily was unmoving, her eyes fixed on his. "And Bill Creed? What did he have to do with it?"

"You'll be pleased to hear that Bill is blissfully unaware. You saw him at Beaumont House as a friend of the family, expressing his concerns. Nothing more, nothing less." Eriksson let out a heavy, exasperated sigh. "Rebecca Briar collected her money and then she did what was best for everyone—she left town."

Confusion filled Emily's mind. She loosened her grip on the letter opener, but only slightly, and eyed the door.

"Say if you're right," she said, "Say if Becky really did leave. What's stopping her from coming after you for more money?"

"Nothing. I imagine I'm at her mercy. But I have the strongest feeling we won't be seeing Rebecca Briar again."

"What about the police? Surely it's a question of time before they discover you've been allowing your son to sell drugs on campus."

Eriksson leaned forward again, eyeing the letter opener still in Emily's hand. "That will depend entirely on you."

"Me?"

"Damien may be ignorant but he's not stupid. He knows to say nothing without a lawyer present. He knows I have the power and the connections to get him out of this mess. Friends in high places will always do right by you if you do right by them, Emily. Quid pro quo, as they say. If only Miss Briar had adhered to this rule. The question is, will you? You can go to the police, tell them everything you've learned. Hell, you can even wheel out Michael Nowak so he can wave his crippled hands. I'll be investigated. My friends in high places will do what they can, but it may not be enough to prevent the story reaching the press, or worse, the university trustees, who, horrified by the risk of a scandal, will request my immediate resignation."

He leaned in closer, his eyes growing dark and fathomless. "Or you could be the wise owl that Bill Creed claims you are, and focus on studying for your finals, which I might remind you are two weeks away. You wouldn't want to ruin your chances now you're so close to qualifying, would you? Not after four years of hard work and a slew of good results and glowing recommendations. It would be a tragedy to throw away a promising career because of someone else's indiscretions, don't you think?"

He smiled then, his eyes unblinking. The threat in his words was all too clear. For someone who had just spent the last ten minutes lambasting the vehement act of blackmail, Vice Chancellor Eriksson, it turned out, was a grand master.

An angry fire burned in Emily's stomach, shooting through her veins.

"Yes," she said, her voice low and trembling, "it would."

Eriksson nodded. Then, as if they had been discussing the weather, he shrugged, picked up the polystyrene cup of coffee, and took a sip.

"It's gone cold."

Emily could not move. Her eyes burned into his.

The Vice Chancellor nodded to the wall clock. "Well, if that's all, you and I both have a lot of work to do. Goodness, on a Saturday too. It's true what they say: no rest for the wicked!"

Emily dropped the letter opener on the desk. She moved in one direction, Vice Chancellor Eriksson in the other.

"Try not to worry too much about Miss Briar," he said, sitting down at his desk and placing the letter opener inside the top drawer. "She's a very resourceful young woman. I'm sure wherever she's ended up, she'll live to fight another day. Now run along, Emily. Time to knuckle down with your studies. I have high hopes for you. Very high hopes indeed."

Slowly, Emily made her way to the door. The Vice Chancellor did not look up again.

Only when Emily had exited the Administration block did she let the tears come. But they were not tears of sadness or worry. They were great, shimmering globules of pure rage.

Vice Chancellor Eriksson had forced her into a corner, and she had let him do so easily. Her feelings for Becky were conflicting and confused. She was risking everything for a person who had lied and cheated and stolen, and who did not care.

Scrubbing her wet face with the back of her hand, Emily strode away. She checked the time—1:04 PM—and quickened her pace. Charlotte would be leaving in less than an hour. That's where her loyalties should lie from now on, Emily thought. With friends that mattered. With friends who cared.

Why then was doubt still eating away at her insides, making her want to scream?

22

DECIDING IT WOULD not be in her best interests to greet Charlotte with a face full of anger, Emily decided to skip the bus and walk home. She would still get there in time to say goodbye to her friend, but first she needed space to process her encounter with Vice Chancellor Eriksson, who had effectively blackmailed her into silence. If she shared what she'd learned with the police, her teaching career would be in ruins before it had begun. Emily had no doubts the Vice Chancellor had the power to make it so, whether he was investigated or not. He had talked about friends in high places. How would she stand a chance if she chose not to keep silent?

If she didn't go to the police, would she be able to live with the consequences? What if Eriksson was lying about Becky? What if he knew exactly where she was, or worse, was responsible for her disappearance?

She wanted to believe him. She wanted to believe Becky really had taken the money and run; that she was in a swanky hotel room somewhere, drinking champagne and laughing at them all.

These thoughts assaulted her mind as she wandered down the high street and across the square. The same bunch of teenagers were lurking on the benches, hoods pulled up despite the hot weather. Shoppers had increased their numbers.

Emily waded through the crowds and entered a winding side street, passing an arcade of shops. Her phone began to ring. Much to her dismay, she saw her mother was calling. She let the phone ring out, adding more guilt to the well.

Halfway down the alley, she came to an abrupt halt. A brightly coloured shop sign had caught her eye.

Rifling in her shoulder bag, she pulled out her wallet and from it, extracted the small roll of receipts she'd taken from Becky's jewellery box. Her gaze moved from the receipts to the shop window. A strange feeling washed over her. Her pulse quickening, Emily marched up to the door, pushed it open, and stepped inside.

Rockin' Roy's Pawn Shop looked like a hoarder's heaven. Cramped aisles brimmed with miscellaneous items whose owners couldn't afford to reclaim them, or had sold them on for a pittance. Emily strode past old television sets, vacuum cleaners, video game consoles, washing machines and musical instruments, making her way to the counter, where an overweight man with thinning hair sat reading a newspaper.

"Hi," Emily said. The man looked up, half surprised to see a customer. His eyes took a leisurely wander down to Emily's breasts. "Are you... Rockin' Roy?"

"The one and only." The man sat up and folded his newspaper in half. "What can I do you for?"

Emily refrained from rolling her eyes. She placed the receipts on the glass counter. "A so-called friend of mine brought in some items a few weeks ago. Some of them didn't exactly belong to her. I was wondering if you could locate the items she brought in—if they're still here, of course."

Roy regarded her for a few seconds, rubbing his stubbly chin.

"It's not my responsibility to make sure everything that comes in here is legit, you know what I'm saying? It's up to people to be honest. If your friend brought in things that don't belong to her, that's between her and whoever she took them from. I'm not breaking no law."

"I'm not suggesting that you are. I'm simply asking if you can locate the items she pawned, so I can look at them."

The shop owner pulled his lips together. His gaze dropped down again, just for a second, but long enough to make Emily clear her throat.

"If there's something belonging to you, you'll have to buy it back. I pay good money for every item that comes in, fair and square."

"But if it's stolen?"

"You'll have to prove it. I run a business here, not a charity."

Emily bit down on her lip. Residual anger left over from her encounter with Vice Chancellor Eriksson still burned in her chest. Rockin' Roy was only adding fuel to the fire.

She forced a smile. "Fine."

Picking up the receipts with thick fingers, Roy sifted through them. He muttered to himself, shot a glance at Emily, and disappeared through a curtained doorway to the right of the counter.

While she waited for him, Emily turned and stared down the aisles. Sunlight illuminated the glass storefront, making the gloom of the pawn shop somehow more miserable. Her gaze fell upon a shelf of soft toys, sat forlornly like abandoned children. Turning back to the counter, she eyed its contents. An array of jewellery was locked inside. Rings of silver, gold, and platinum. Bracelets, necklaces, a pair of diamond earrings.

Emily heaved her shoulders. Rockin' Roy's Pawn Shop was not helping her mood. How could she have been so wrong about Becky? Yes, she knew she was troubled, but to know she had deliberately set out to hurt people—even if some of those people had deserved it—made Emily question her own judge of character. And what was she doing here anyway? The only answer she could come up with was good, old fashioned instinct.

The curtain slid back and Roy returned, carrying a large red folder.

"Inventory," he muttered, this time barely making eye contact. Dumping the folder on the counter, he opened it up, licked his finger and thumb, and leafed through the enclosed documents. Occasionally, his gaze shifted to the receipts. After two minutes of uncomfortable silence, Roy looked up.

"So?" Emily said, leaning over to observe his handwritten scrawl.

Roy pulled the inventory folder away. He regarded her for a second, his brow folding into several creases.

"You're not the cops, are you? Because I told you, it's people's responsibility not to bring in stolen goods. I've done nothing wrong."

Emily told him she was a mere student, and resisted snatching the folder away from him to find out for herself what Becky had pawned.

"Fine then," Rockin' Roy said. He cleared his throat and

began listing the items. "One HP Windows 10 laptop. Black. Eight gigabytes of RAM, five hundred-"

"Got it. Next." The laptop was Becky's. Emily had noticed it missing from her room.

"One silver charm bracelet with four charms. The charms listed as follows: a cat, a love heart, a skull, and-"

"A serpent." Also Becky's. It was her favourite, which she'd worn all the time. "What's next?"

"One men's wrist watch. Armani. Black and gold. A very nice piece indeed. I remember that. Sold it on eBay for a pretty penny."

"You sold it? Exactly how long do you give your customers to pay back their loans?"

Roy glared at her. "Ninety days. Except your friend didn't pawn it. She sold it outright. See?"

He thrust the receipt under her nose. Emily dreaded to think how the watch had come into Becky's possession. The same thought passed through her mind as Roy reeled off the next two items: one unused patent leather wallet, and a pair of Tiffany pearl earrings.

"Last one," the pawnbroker said, waving the final receipt. His finger scrolled down the inventory list. "Ah yes, here we go…"

As Roy read out the item's description, Emily's breath caught in her throat. "Pardon me?"

Roy repeated himself. He looked up from the folder, frowning. "That yours, is it?"

Emily was lost in a collision of confused thoughts. *It couldn't be.*

"So, will you be wanting to buy that back, then?" Roy stared down at the counter and tapped the glass. "I've got it right here."

Emily followed his gaze. The room spun around her, forcing her to grip the counter. Roy stared at her with raised eyebrows.

She glanced back down at the counter. Seconds passed before she found her voice again.

"How much for it?" she asked.

23

EMILY COULD HEAR the shouts and grunts of the removal men as she raced into the street. She had run almost the entire way, and was breathless and sweating. Darting past two men in matching blue overalls, she hurried down the garden path and into the house. Another man was inside, grappling with a heavy looking box.

Charlotte was in the kitchen, last-minute packing the contents of her food cupboard. When she saw Emily, she rose and flashed her an angry glare.

"You said you were going to be here," she grunted. "It's after two. You know I didn't want to be left alone in the house with these guys."

Emily stared at her. She looked as if she might cry. Behind them, two of the men entered the hall and headed into the living room.

"Just the red armchair in the corner please!" Charlotte called out to them. "The one with the label!"

The men nodded and disappeared. Charlotte returned her focus to Emily.

"Honestly, Em, I'm really annoyed. What are you doing going to see Michael Nowak? I thought I was about to say goodbye to an empty house. What did he say anyway?"

She turned to put more food items in the box.

Emily watched her, remembering the Vice Chancellor's warning.

"Not much," she said.

Charlotte hefted the box onto the counter. Out in the hall, the men had emerged from the living room and were now carrying the red armchair to the front door.

"Careful, please!" Charlotte snapped. She stared at Emily, catching the expression on her face. "What? It's a family heirloom."

Emily nodded.

She produced the silver necklace from her pocket and held it up. "You mean, like this?"

The colour drained from Charlotte's face. Her mouth fell open. The crucifix dangled from the chain, reflecting light into her pupils.

"New era, new you: that's what you said." Emily could feel the anger rising. "You told me you'd put it away in your keepsake box, a memory to always treasure but not to wear around your neck like a stone."

Charlotte's fingers touched the empty space where her collarbones met. She swallowed. Hard.

"I...I did," she said. "Where did you find it?"

She reached for the crucifix. Emily snatched it away.

"From Rockin' Roy's Pawn Shop. It was there along with a bunch of other items that Becky sold."

"And you bought it back for me?" Charlotte's gaze met Emily's. She tried to smile. "Emily, I don't know what to say."

"How about you tell me what happened between you and Becky," Emily said, all trace of patience vanished. "How about you tell me where she is."

Charlotte shook her head. "I don't know."

"Don't lie to me, Charlotte! This necklace was the only thing you had belonging to your mother. You told me you'd worn it every day since she died, that you'd never take it off. Becky took it from you, didn't she? She made you give it up and she sold it to a pawn shop. She didn't even get that much for it. I thought it was strange when you'd stopped wearing it. You've been lying this whole time. Pretending everything's okay."

Charlotte's face had turned a strange colour. Her eyes shot from Emily, to the crucifix still dangling from Emily's hand, to the hall, where the removal men were milling up and down. Tears stung her eyes. She blinked them away.

"She must have taken it from me," she said. "She must have taken it from my memory box."

"Stop lying!"

Emily knew it was true. She could see it in the wideness of Charlotte's eyes, the way her fingers twitched and her chest heaved.

"I have to go," Charlotte muttered. "I don't have time for this nonsense."

She moved toward the door. Emily blocked her path.

"Charlotte, what happened?"

"I don't know anything. Let me go!"

The anger Emily had been trying to contain suddenly exploded.

"For God's sake, Charlotte! Stop lying! What is it? Was Becky blackmailing you, too?"

Charlotte stopped in her tracks.

"She was, wasn't she?" Emily realised. "Along with Councillor Beaumont and Vice Chancellor Eriksson, and God knows who else."

Tears splashed down Charlotte's face.

"Please, Charlotte," Emily softened her voice. "What could Becky possibly have on you?"

Tears turned into great sobs. Charlotte buried her face into her hands.

"I didn't mean to do it," she wailed. "I just wanted to be left alone."

A chill crawled over Emily's skin.

"She kept pushing. Asking for more money I didn't have. She was going to show it to him!"

"Charlotte! What did you do?"

Charlotte sucked in a breath and closed her eyes. Her sobs quietened. Her body went very still.

Emily tightened her grip on the crucifix.

"Charlotte," she repeated. "Where's Becky?"

Charlotte opened her eyes. When Emily stared into them, she saw empty space.

An awkward cough drew her attention to the doorway behind. One of the removal men stared at the space between them, doing his best not to acknowledge Charlotte's tear-stained face or the heavy atmosphere, thick as treacle, smothering the kitchen.

"We're about done, here," he said. "We'll start heading off."

He waited for one of the women to say something. When neither of them spoke, he shrugged a shoulder and turned back to the hall. He was halfway down when Charlotte called out.

"Can you wait an hour? Take a break or something before you head off."

The man hovered. "We can. We'll have to charge for the extra time."

Charlotte nodded.

Satisfied, the man left them alone.

Charlotte looked up, meeting Emily's frightened gaze.

"It's not far," she said. "We can take my car."

24

THEY DROVE IN silence, leaving the town behind and disappearing into the countryside, further and further away from people. Despite Emily's efforts, Charlotte had not uttered a word since leaving the kitchen. She kept her eyes on the road and her foot pressed on the accelerator. Emily sat in the passenger seat, fingers tapping on her knees. Becky had been missing for five days now. She had no idea if she was alive or dead.

Emily stole a quick glance at Charlotte. Her skin was slick with perspiration, giving it a marble-like sheen. Her expression sat somewhere between shock and terror. She wondered what was going through her mind. Nothing good; of that she was sure.

Ten minutes passed. The car turned off the main road and plunged down a narrow track. Tall hedgerows closed in on both sides. Centimetres lay between them and the car.

"Where are we going?" Emily asked, her shoulder muscles knotting. Charlotte remained silent. The road began to snake and buck, veering off to the left then the right, each corner sharper than the next. "Can you at least tell me if I'm going to find Becky alive or…"

She couldn't finish the sentence. Charlotte tightened her grip on the wheel.

At last, the track came to an end, merging with a two-lane road. Charlotte took a left, then another right. The car disappeared down another track, this one even narrower than the last.

Emily could feel anxiety spreading through her body like sickness. She made sure Charlotte wasn't looking then pulled out her phone. To her dismay, she saw there was no signal. She was out here alone with Charlotte, driving into the unknown. An hour ago, Charlotte had been her friend; quiet and intelligent, with a wry sense of humour and a benevolent aura. Now, she was afraid of her.

It occurred to Emily that she had spent the last year living with total strangers. The people she thought she had known were gone now. In their place, were two shadowy figures, twisted by anguish and anger and despair.

Charlotte spun the wheel, turning the car onto a dirt road. Trees appeared on both sides, plunging the world into shadows. Emily wondered if she'd made a terrible mistake coming along on this journey.

A minute later, the road ended in a wide, round clearing, surrounded by forest.

Charlotte slowed the car to a halt and turned off the engine. For a long time, she sat unmoving, staring through the windscreen, face devoid of expression. Just as the silence became unbearable and Emily's anxiety reached excruciating levels, Charlotte grabbed the door handle and pushed the door open.

"Come on." Without looking back, she stepped out of the car.

The sun had been smothered by a growing formation of clouds, teasing goose pimples to the surface of Emily's flesh. She closed the door and stood by the car, staring into the trees. On the other side, Charlotte nodded.

"It's this way."

She began walking toward the forest. Emily watched her for a few seconds. No shovel, she thought. At least they wouldn't be digging anyone up. She glanced around, searching the ground. Finding a fist sized rock, she slipped it into her jacket pocket. *Just in case.*

Charlotte was waiting for her at the tree line. She waited until Emily was two metres away, then disappeared into the forest.

It was unusually quiet. The canopy above their heads was bereft of birds. Foliage crunched beneath Emily's feet. She was having trouble breathing.

They walked along a worn trail that curled between the tree trunks. It was a natural trail, worn into the ground over time by either human or animal feet. Emily's eyes were fixed on Charlotte's back. Occasionally, her gaze would stray off to the sides, noting that the deeper they were heading into the forest, the darker it was becoming.

"Where are we going?" Emily's voice bounced off the trees. Charlotte ploughed ahead, her movements stiff and zombie-like. "Damn it! Will you talk to me?"

The path turned. Charlotte stepped off it, heading for a thick copse of silver birch trees.

Emily stared at the path beneath her feet. She did not want to leave it.

Charlotte had quickened her pace and was now several metres ahead. Emily called after her. She broke into a jog, quickly catching up.

"Hey, I'm talking to you," she panted.

Charlotte rounded the birch trees and made for a large cluster of undergrowth. The ground grew boggy beneath their feet. Wet soil splashed on their clothes. Emily lunged forward. She grabbed Charlotte's arm, spinning her around.

For the first time since they'd left the house, Charlotte met her gaze. Emily gasped. It was as if she'd aged ten years during their car journey. Her eyes had grown round and dull. Shadows swam beneath them. This is what guilt does to you, Emily thought, and a sudden unpleasant chill slipped beneath her jacket.

Charlotte turned to get moving again but Emily held fast.

"You need to talk to me, right now," she said. "You need to tell me what happened with Becky. You need to tell me if...if we're about to find her alive or dead."

Charlotte stared at her blankly. She blinked a couple of times, as if she'd just woken up.

"I slept with Damien," she said.

Emily was shocked. "What? When?"

"I don't know, sometime last year. We got talking in the bar. I knew who he was, what he did. But I didn't care. It was just a drunken one night stand, nothing more. A bit of fun."

Emily shook her head.

"Everyone does it," Charlotte said defensively. "I can't be the priest's daughter twenty-four seven."

"I'm not judging you. I'm confused. What does sleeping with Damien Harris a year ago have to do with Becky?"

Charlotte stared off into the trees. "One night, a couple months ago, Becky came to my room. She was high as a kite, swaying everywhere, chewing her face off. She told me she'd been with Damien Harris. That she'd been hanging out with him a lot. That afternoon, she'd been at his flat. He'd had to slip out for half an hour and he'd let her stay.

She was using his computer and decided to snoop around. She found . . . videos."

"What kind of videos?"

Charlotte started at the ground. "It turns out Damien likes to record the women he sleeps with. Secretly. Without them knowing. Apparently, he has a whole collection on his hard drive. I had no idea that he'd. . ."

Charlotte was silent. Her face had turned deep red.

"I'm sorry," Emily said.

"At first, I didn't believe Becky. Then she showed me the video. She'd copied it to her phone. She said she wanted money. She said if I didn't give it to her, she'd make sure that video was uploaded to the Internet for everyone to see. I begged her. I pleaded with her. She just laughed and said she'd send it to my father, too." Charlotte continued to stare in her strange way, her voice slow and emotionless, as if she were reading from a script. "I knew it would kill him. He's a priest. You know what his beliefs are. After Mum died, it was just the two of us. We'd never been best friends but he was all I had. If he saw that video. . . If the church found out, or the community, anyone. . . I wouldn't have been able to live with myself. So, I gave Becky her money."

"And she deleted the video?"

Charlotte shook her head. "A week later she came back, demanding more. Then the week after that. Then the week after that. Until I had no money left to give her." Charlotte reached for the empty space around her neck. "That's when she took my necklace."

Emily still had the crucifix in her pocket, not wanting to return it until she knew the rest of the story.

"It was all that was left of my mum. Becky knew that but she took it anyway. And I let her."

"Why didn't you come to me? Why didn't you tell me what was going on?"

"And what would you have done?" Charlotte's voice was sharp and bitter. "That video would have been all over the Internet in a second. She would have sent it to my dad. Even if I managed to get hold of the original video, Becky had already made at least one copy. What was to stop her from making more?"

"What about Monday night?" Emily said, quietly. "Where do you come into it?"

For the briefest of moments, rage flashed like lighting across Charlotte's face. Then blankness returned.

"She called me. She told me she was leaving town and I would never hear from her again. But she wanted one last favour. That was the word she used—*favour*. She gave me a list of things she wanted from her room. I was to pack them and bring them to the station, and I had thirty minutes in which to do it." Charlotte hesitated, looking back over her shoulder. "I packed her bag for her. I drove to the station. She was waiting for me when I pulled up in the parking space around the back. It was dark. No one was around. I gave her the damn bag and I thought that would be the end of it.

"Then she said she had time to kill before her train arrived. She started boasting about all the people she'd exploited. About all the money she'd taken from them. She was boasting to me—one of the people she'd stolen from. Then she started laughing about how she'd pulled a fast one on Damien."

"Because she owed him money?"

Charlotte shook her head. "Didn't you work that out? Damien was in on it from the beginning. They chose their targets together. He helped plan everything. She said he even told her what to say when it came to blackmailing his father. She was laughing that night because she had no intention of sharing the money with Damien. She played him like an idiot."

Emily was stunned. When Damien had told her Becky owed him money, he'd meant his share of the takings. Had he been hoping Emily would track Becky down, leading him straight to her? As for Vice Chancellor Eriksson, he had no idea his son was jointly responsible for his blackmail. It was clever of Damien, she supposed. He'd found a way of punishing his father without him ever knowing. She turned back to Charlotte, who was staring into space through red-rimmed eyes. "What happened next?"

"She kept going on and on," Charlotte said, her voice barely above a whisper. "About how bloody clever she was. About how she was going to start a new life where nobody knew her thanks to the money everyone had kindly handed over. Something in me snapped. I thought: what happens when the money runs out? Who will she come for then? As long as she had that video, she could call at any time and demand more. It could go on forever." Her hands began to tremble. She held them up, staring at them. "All her talk was giving me a headache. I remember thinking: I wish she would just shut up. But she wouldn't stop. I couldn't bear it. So, I made her stop."

The temperature had dropped. A breeze blew up around them and continued through the forest. Emily gripped the rock in her pocket.

"Charlotte, what did you do? Where's Becky?"

Charlotte stared at her open-mouthed. A lone tear

splashed down her cheek.

"She's this way," she said, and took off once more.

This time, Emily stayed by her side. They rounded a large crop of ferns. The ground began to descend sharply. Charlotte stopped still. She stood, swaying like a flower on the breeze. Then, rather than head down the slope, she turned right, and walked another few metres, coming to a halt by a pile of fallen branches.

"Here," she said, looking back at Emily. "She's here."

Confused, Emily peered at the ground. "Where?"

Charlotte pointed. Emily peered over the fallen branches.

"She's down there."

Emily stared at the rusted metal hatch with mounting horror. "What is this?"

"An old bunker left over from the Second World War. People used to live in it. Did you know there are bunkers all over the country? Hidden beneath cities and in the countryside, even buried in people's back yards—protection from the bombs dropped by Nazi warplanes. We came here on a field trip in my first year. It got condemned not long after. All they did was chain it up." She tapped the hatch with her foot. There was no chain on it now. "No one ever comes out this way, so…"

Her shoes sinking into wet mud, Emily crouched down beside the hatch. She ran fingers along its edges. Rust crumbled into dust. Images of Becky's broken body lying in the dark haunted her mind.

"You brought her all the way out here?" she asked, without turning around.

Charlotte took a step closer. "I don't really remember it. Something must have triggered in my brain. A memory. I must have thought: no one will find her here."

Another image came to Emily: Charlotte dragging Becky's unconscious body through the forest at night.

"I thought I'd killed her. She was bleeding. She wouldn't wake up." Charlotte scuffed the ground with her foot. "It was like a dream."

Emily was gripped by a surge of panic. While they were up here talking, Becky was down there in the dark. Her fingers shot toward the opening mechanism. She gripped the lever with both hands. It wouldn't move.

"How do I open this thing?" she said.

Charlotte was leaning over her, watching her through curious eyes. "It's rusty. You have to put your strength into it."

With the ground wet from yesterday's rain, it was hard for Emily to anchor herself. She tugged on the lever. Her feet slipped from beneath her and she landed on her side. Hoisting herself up into a crouch, she tried a different approach, placing her heels on the edge of the hatch.

This time she did not slip. Clenching her teeth, she pulled on the lever again. A metallic grating filled her ears. The lever shot toward her. Emily tumbled onto her back.

The hatch door was unlocked.

Getting up, she moved around to the other side of the hatch, crouched down, and gripped the edges of the door. She pushed up, surprised by how heavy it was.

Charlotte had moved to the side but made no effort to help.

Emily shifted her weight, channelled her strength into her arms, and lifted.

The hatch door flew open.

She found herself staring into a void of impenetrable

darkness. It caught her off balance, making her blood freeze.

A ladder descended into the depths below, rusty and slippery-looking. Fear crawled up through the blackness.

"She's down there?" Emily said, her throat drying.

Charlotte crouched down. She nodded as she slipped her hand inside her pocket and took out a small torch. She handed it to Emily.

Depressing the power button, Emily made sure she had a tight grip on the edge of the hatch then leaned over. She pointed the torch beam downward. The light splashed on the ladder rungs, illuminating rust and lichen and droplets of water. It wasn't a huge drop, perhaps about three metres. But it was not the drop that scared Emily. It was what lay beyond it, down there in the dark.

Keeping a watchful eye on Charlotte, Emily leaned a little further into the hole. She tightened her grip on the side of the hatch. She lowered her other arm into the darkness. The torch beam moved down the ladder. She could just make out the ground below, which was hard and wet. She caught her breath. At the periphery of the torchlight, she saw a pair of feet, one of them bare. She changed the angle of the torch and the feet grew legs. The left leg was dark and bloody.

"I see her," Emily said. "I see Becky."

Charlotte nodded, her expression devoid of emotion.

"We need to get down there." An awful image flashed in Emily's mind: Becky's body crashing against the ladder, pitching through darkness. "You go first."

Charlotte remained frozen in a crouch, staring into the bunker.

"I'm not even kidding," Emily barked. "Go. Now!"

Terror crept over Charlotte's face. At last, she nodded. Crossing herself, she gripped both sides of the hatch and slowly lowered herself in. Emily watched her cling to the ladder with shaking hands and then take a step down. The ladder trembled, sending rusty flakes drifting to the depths below.

Emily gave the hatch door a push. Satisfied it wasn't going to flip over and seal them in, she clenched the torch between her teeth. Then, sucking in an unsteady breath, she lowered herself into darkness.

25

PANIC KICKED IN as soon as Emily began to descend the ladder, growing stronger as she moved deeper and deeper into darkness. With the torch clamped between her teeth, she had to rely on the daylight seeping in from above. Charlotte had already reached the bottom and was now standing by the foot of the ladder, swaying from side to side and making no attempt to rush to Becky's aid.

Emily increased the speed of her descent but succeeded in slipping on a wet and mossy rung. For a terrifying second, she dangled in the darkness by one hand. She cried out. The torch slipped from her mouth, bouncing off the ladder and hitting the ground next to Charlotte, who made no move to pick it up. By some miracle, the bulb did not shatter.

Emily swung herself toward the ladder. Her feet and hands now safely back on the rungs, she continued downward.

When she reached the ground a few seconds later, Charlotte had still not moved. Emily pointed the torch at the body on the floor.

"Becky," she whispered.

She was by her side in a second, crouched over, two fingers pressed into Becky's jugular.

"She's alive!"

She shot a glance at Charlotte who, caught between darkness and light, looked grey and sickly, her eyes two unseeing hollows. Setting the torch on the ground, Emily lifted Becky's head into her lap and examined the damage. The hair on the right side was matted together with dried blood. More blood caked her face.

A noise came from Becky's throat, low and guttural. Her eyes rolled beneath their lids.

"Becky? Can you hear me? It's Emily. You're safe."

Becky's eyelids flickered open. Her pupils were two small points. Emily called her name again, raising her voice. Becky's gaze locked onto her own. She looked up at Emily through a veil of confusion.

"Em. . ."

"Don't speak. We're going to get you out of here. We're going to take you to a hospital."

"No . . . hosp. . ." Becky's voice trailed off. She was losing focus again.

Emily tapped her gently on the cheek. Her breathing didn't sound right. Her cracked lips were tinted blue.

Pulling out her phone, Emily yelled with frustration to see there was still no signal.

The ladder was the only way out. But how were they going to get her up it?

Becky's eyes were closing again. Emily gave her a short, sharp shake.

"Stay with me, Becky. You have to stay awake."

Becky opened her eyes.

"Thirsty," she croaked.

"We need to get her help, now," Emily said to Charlotte. She looked up. "Charlotte?"

But Charlotte was no longer standing by the ladder. She was halfway up it, climbing back to the surface.

"Charlotte!"

Emily froze, watching her make the ascent. She was moving slowly but with every passing second, she was heading closer to the light. Emily moved quickly, laying Becky on the ground.

"I'll be back!" she called, racing toward the ladder. "I promise!"

Reaching up, Emily began to climb.

Charlotte was a metre and a half ahead of her. Daylight bathed her body.

Emily climbed faster. Her feet slipped in water but her hands were iron grips. Finding her footing again, she continued to climb.

Charlotte reached the top of the ladder and hoisted herself out.

A cry escaped Emily's mouth. She pulled herself up, hand over hand, foot over foot. She was a metre away from the top.

Charlotte was on her knees, hanging over the edge and catching her breath.

Their eyes locked, just for a second. Charlotte stumbled to her feet.

"Charlotte, no!" Emily hauled herself up. Her hand grasped the top rung.

She looked up in time to see Charlotte heave the hatch door up and over.

"I'm sorry!" she wailed.

The hatch door came crashing down.

26

THE ROCK.

Emily's fingers wrapped around it, tearing it from her pocket. She slammed it down on the edge of the hatch, just as the door came smashing down. The crack of metal landing hard at close range was deafening. Emily shrieked and almost lost her grip.

She looked up. The rock had smashed but a small part of it remained, creating a wedge in between the hatch door and the rim, preventing it from sealing shut.

Instinct took over. Gripping the ladder with both hands, Emily forced her feet up a rung. Then another, until she was hunched up like a clam, her back pressed against the hatch door.

She pushed up, channelling her adrenaline-fuelled strength into her back. The hatch door lifted a few centimetres. She straightened her body, pushing up with her shoulders.

The door opened far enough for her to get an arm through.

She pushed up, heaving her shoulder against the door.

Emily emitted a desperate cry, her body clenched between the metal above and below, and launched herself upward one final time.

The door opened ninety degrees, pivoted momentarily, then gravity took care of the rest.

Light rushed in. Emily grabbed both sides of the hatch. She dangled there for a second, nothing but empty space beneath her. Lifting her legs, she swung them over and rolled onto solid ground.

She gave herself half a second to recover and staggered to her feet.

Charlotte was already on the trail. She had stopped still, terrified eyes fixed on Emily.

Emily stumbled forward, picking up speed.

Charlotte turned and bolted. She was heading out of the forest, back to the car. She was going to get away.

Emily's feet hit the trail, kicking foliage into the air. She pumped her legs and arms, and ducked her head. She raced forward. The edge of the forest came up to meet her. She burst through, heading straight for the car.

Charlotte was at the driver door, keys in hand.

Emily raced up behind her, stumbled into a pothole, and flew forward.

Her body slammed into Charlotte's.

They hit the ground and rolled.

Emily was first on her feet. The car keys lay in a pool of muddy water. She lunged forward, sweeping them up. She spun on her heels. Her chest heaved up and down. Her lungs burned.

Charlotte sat on with her legs splayed in front of her like a toddler.

The two remained rooted to the ground, catching their breaths.

Charlotte began to cry.

"I'm sorry," she moaned. Tears flooded her face.

Emily heaved her shoulders. She was furious. "For leaving Becky for dead or for trying to turn me into Tutan-bloody-khamun?"

Charlotte wiped her tears. More came. "What happens now? Will you call the police?"

The car keys were clenched in Emily's fist. "We can talk about that later," she said between breaths. "Right now, you're going to help me get Becky out of that hole." She stabbed a finger at Charlotte. "And no more funny business."

Perhaps she was wrong to trust Charlotte but Emily had little choice. Grabbing bottled water from the car, she hurried back to the bunker. Charlotte followed behind like a scolded child. Reaching the hatch, Emily stared into darkness once more.

"I don't know how we're going to get her out," she said, unable to disguise the panic in her voice. Even if she had the strength to carry Charlotte in a fireman's lift over her shoulder, there was no way she could get her up the ladder. The alternative was to drive until she had a phone signal, then call for the emergency services. But there was no chance in hell she would leave Becky alone with Charlotte, and no way she was trusting Charlotte to be the one to go for help.

"There's another way," Charlotte said, as if reading Emily's mind. She had turned and was peering down the slope at the forest floor below. "Another door. You can-"

"Show me."

Grabbing Charlotte by the arm, Emily plunged down the slope. They found the door a few seconds later, covered up with broken branches. Once they had removed them, they were faced with a padlocked chain.

Emily looked around on the ground, found another rock, and brought it crashing down. The chain, which was weakened and rusty, snapped on impact.

The door was open. Light flooded the bunker.

"You're first," Emily said, nudging Charlotte with her arm.

Charlotte nodded, there but not *really* there.

It didn't take long to find Becky. She was barely conscious.

Emily made Charlotte scoop up her head and feed her a bottle of water in slow sips, while she assessed the rest of the damage.

She was no doctor but the way Becky's ankle had swollen like a balloon, it was reasonable to assume it was broken. Her left arm and hand, too. Emily wondered how she had survived for so long down here in this dank, terrifying place.

Once the water bottle had been drained, Emily removed her jacket and used it to secure Becky's legs just below the knees.

"We're going to carry her," she said.

Guilt soured Charlotte's features. "Will she live?"

Emily stared at Becky's now unconscious form, unable to answer.

It was another ten long, painful minutes before the two emerged from the forest, carrying Becky stretcher-like between them.

Reaching the car, Emily hit the remote unlock button on the keys, and together they hoisted her gently into the back seat.

"I'll drive," Emily said.

Charlotte drooped her shoulders and nodded.

The engine started on the first attempt. Emily made a three-point turn, glancing at Charlotte, who sat with Becky's head resting in her lap, then drove them away from the forest.

They reached the hospital thirty minutes later. Emily parked up and killed the engine. She twisted around to face her passengers. Apart from the muddy smears on her face, Charlotte was as pale as cotton. Becky was a mess of dirt and dried blood and matted hair. Her eyes were still shut.

A decision needed to be made. Emily didn't want to be the one to make it.

"The way I see it," she said, glancing out the window, "you have two choices. One: we go in there, tell them exactly what happened, and you both deal with the consequences of police involvement. I think we all know the outcome isn't going to be good for either of you."

She let the thought rest for a moment.

Charlotte began to cry. "I don't want to go to prison."

"Or two: you come up with a story about how you happened to find Becky in this state and then hope to God that 'A', she doesn't screw it all up when she's conscious and 'B', she doesn't go ahead and share your night of passion to the world anyway."

A strange looked passed over Charlotte's face. "Where would I have found her?"

"Use your imagination." Irritation crept into Emily's voice. She was furious with them both. "You've done terrible things to each other. It doesn't matter who did what first." Charlotte began to protest. Emily silenced her with a cutting glare. "I'm sorry, Charlotte, but you lost that right when you beat Becky half to death and threw her into an abandoned bunker. You were about to move away without telling anyone what happened. And did I mention the part where you tried to lock me in there with her? That's two counts of attempted murder."

The realisation of what Charlotte had tried to do was only now hitting her, leaving her nauseous and panicked. "I honestly can't decide which of you is worse. But the fact remains, if either one of you speak out, you'll both be facing criminal charges, probably prison sentences." Emily let out a deep sigh. Suddenly, she felt exhausted. "Those are your choices. Choose quickly because either way, Becky is getting medical treatment whether you think she deserves it or not."

Feeling spent, she took the keys out of the ignition and passed them back to Charlotte. All she wanted was to go home, take a hot shower and scrub herself clean. The events of this past week had left an indelible stain that would sully her mind each time she reminisced about her university days. As strange as it seemed, it pissed her off more than Charlotte trying to kill her.

She glanced in the rear-view mirror, catching the wretched expression on Charlotte's face.

"Why would you help me? Why aren't you calling the police?" she croaked.

It was a good question, and one Emily was asking herself right now. She supposed that, despite Charlotte's actions, she pitied her. Becky had forced her into an unbearable situation. She had pushed her to the edge of reason and then pushed again, until Charlotte had snapped and retaliated. It seemed to Emily that Charlotte had been running scared ever since, her actions driven by shock and terror. Did she deserve to go to prison? Possibly. But would any of them be sitting here right now if Becky hadn't played Charlotte that tape and demanded money in exchange for silence?

Charlotte, Becky, Damien Harris, Vice Chancellor Eriksson, Councillor Beaumont—they had all committed punishable crimes. And yet, in one form or another, they were all already paying for their actions.

"One, turn yourself in," she repeated, tiredly shaking her head. "Or two, make up a story."

A voice, cracked and gravelly from dehydration, disturbed the silence. "Or three. . ." —Emily spun around to see Becky had opened her eyes and was staring up at Charlotte— "you leave me at the door and you drive away. Maybe then . . . we'll both . . . avoid getting arrested."

Slowly, she turned her head in Emily's direction.

"Why, Becky?" Emily gasped. "Why have you done all these terrible things?"

Becky's eyelids fluttered.

"Why not?" she said.

A minute later, they were out of the car and carrying Becky's unconscious body through the hospital doors. Emily hung back as a nurse came rushing to Becky's aid. She didn't wait to see what happened next. She glanced down at her filthy clothes. The hospital doors slid open and she walked through them.

Stopping by Charlotte's car, she dug a hand into her pocket and pulled out the silver crucifix. Emily stared at it sitting on the palm of her hand. She slipped it over one of the windscreen wipers and headed to the exit.

She'd walked a few metres when the hospital doors

opened and Charlotte came hurrying out. She glanced up, catching Emily's eye. A look passed between them: a collision of guilt and anger and betrayal. Then, Emily turned and walked through the gates, in search of a bus to take her home.

27

THE WEEKEND CAME and went with Emily sat at her desk. The time she'd spent searching for Becky had put her seriously behind with her studies. Her final exams were now less than two weeks away. Emily stayed away from the hospital. She felt guilty for dumping Becky there like an unwanted dog, and conflicted for not reporting anything to the police, but she had her future to think about, and right now, she was in danger of screwing it all up.

She had not heard from Charlotte again. She thought it was probably for the best. Becky was alive. Whatever new web of lies she'd spun had obviously done the trick. It wasn't until Becky's mother showed up at the house on Monday morning, announcing she was here to pack up Becky's room, that Emily learned 'where' Becky had been all this time.

"Mugged and left for dead!" Mrs Briar said, as she unfolded flat pack boxes. "She doesn't remember anything. Just arriving at the station to take a train home, then stepping outside for a cigarette, and being accosted by two men. I always told her smoking was a dangerous habit. If only she could recall what those animals looked like. She'd been unconscious out in that wasteland behind the station for days. Where were the station staff? That's what I want to know. Thank God, she finally woke up! Thank God that girl found her wandering the streets! A proper Good Samaritan, she was. Disappeared before the nurses could even get her name…"

It was a believable story, Emily supposed, if you didn't overthink it.

"Well, Becky will be coming home with us where she'll be safe. Besides, from what I hear, she won't be graduating this year. I had no idea she was failing. What a disappointment!"

The removal men came the next day.

The rest of the week rushed by. Emily delivered her final classes to her cohort of young students. On Friday, they gave her cards and presents, and Principal Talbot gave her a special mention in the school assembly. He called her into his office later that afternoon, asking if she'd made a decision about his job offer. Emily told him that she had.

The rest of her time was spent poring over books and online resources. Her mother called several times, anxiously demanding to know if her only child would be returning home.

"Mrs Skinner says there's a job for you over in Bishopstown if you want it. Needs someone to teach the Year Sevens. Says you should call her and arrange an interview."

"But I—"

"And that Hemmingway boy has been asking about you again. Wants to know when you're back."

"Lewis?"

"He's sweet on you. But there's plenty of time for that kind of thing once you're settled at the school."

Angela Jackson, who had decided she was speaking to

Emily again, called the night before the exams. Becky had been discharged from the hospital. Loretta Cartwright, whoever that was, had seen her in a car with her mother. And speaking of cars, was Emily at all interested in buying Angela's VW as she had decided to sell poor Bessie before heading off to Tanzania for six months where she would be teaching English to orphans. Emily told her she would think about it.

Hanging up, Emily stood and stretched her spine, enjoying the popping sensation of her disks after hours hunched over her desk. She wandered downstairs and made some tea. She'd grown quite accustomed to having the house to herself. In fact, in light of recent experiences, she'd vowed never to share her home with anyone else ever again.

Her thoughts turned to the exams. Soon, they would all be over. Then, that would be it: the end of her life as a student and the beginning of something else entirely. The thought brought on an immediate headache and she went straight to bed.

The day of her finals arrived. Emily showered, dressed, and ate an energy-filled breakfast of oats and blueberries. She used the walk to the campus to clear her mind of thoughts outside the arena of educational studies.

Angela was waiting for her in the quad, nervously pacing up and down, sucking on a cigarette.

"Since when do you smoke?" Emily asked.

Angela shrugged. "Since just now. I can't believe we're finally here. God, I'm going to have a nervous breakdown, I swear."

"You'll be fine. Just breathe."

It was almost time.

They headed to the examinations hall, Angela filling the journey with anxious chatter. Neither of them mentioned Becky Briar, as if the mere utterance of her name would bring them immediate bad luck. In fact, Emily thought, I'd quite like it if I never had to speak her name again.

Arriving at the main doors, Angela fell silent and squeezed Emily's hand.

"Good luck."

Emily squeezed back. "Good luck."

A few hours later and it was all over. Emily stepped out into the sunshine feeling frazzled and exhausted. Angela appeared beside her, looking as if she'd been pulled from a car wreck.

"One down," she said.

Parting ways, Emily strolled back to the gates. All she wanted now was to go home, eat ice cream, and prepare for the next exam. She was just about to do exactly that when a deep, masculine voice called her name. She looked up to see Vice Chancellor Eriksson.

He walked toward her at a deliberate pace.

"How was it?" he asked, blocking her path.

Emily eyed him warily. "Fine."

Eriksson nodded. He looked over Emily's shoulder, then to his left and right. "I hear a mutual acquaintance of ours has flown back to the nest."

"With all of your money."

The Vice Chancellor's face flushed scarlet. "Have you heard anything?"

She regarded him for a moment before shaking her head. "Only that your son was released without charge. He really does have some friends in high places, doesn't he?"

The Vice Chancellor's eyes grew wide and round at the word *son*. He looked over Emily's shoulder. "He's been very lucky. He's agreed to move back with his mother for a little while. University life, it seems, is not for everybody."

"No, I suppose it's not."

Eriksson leaned in closer. When he spoke again, his voice was hushed and tinged with anxiety. "And what about you, Emily? Have you decided what you're going to do?"

She stared at him, deliberately, for a long time. "As a matter of fact, I have."

With that, she strolled past him.

"Well, whatever you've decided," Eriksson called after her, "I hope for your sake it's the right decision."

A small group of students walked by. Emily came to a halt.

"By the way," she called over her shoulder. "The next time you speak to your son, perhaps you might have a word with him about the ethics of filming his sexual conquests without their consent. I'm sure that sort of thing is against the law."

By the time Emily reached the university gates, a heaviness had settled on her shoulders. It was still with her when she returned home and began studying for her next exam.

As she worked, her mind occasionally drifted off, taking her to tropical beaches and along rainforest trails. She pictured herself travelling from country to country with just a bag on her back. It was a nice daydream, one that kept her distracted for the rest of the afternoon.

Cornwall, England
July

28

THE OLD VW coughed and spluttered as it pulled up outside of a small white cottage that sat in an overgrown garden.

Emily was motionless behind the wheel, her heart thumping in her chest as she assessed the neglect the garden had fallen into. It pained her. She had spent hours in spring pruning and clipping and sculpting, hoping the view from the window would bring some joy. Heaving her shoulders, she turned and looked along the road. Other cottages in nicely kept gardens lined both sides. She could only imagine what the neighbours had to say about this eyesore at the end of the street.

It was Sunday morning, almost midday. A large portion of the village would be in church, singing hymns and praising Jesus, while chickens roasted in ovens, the temperature turned down low so as not to dry the meat.

Nothing had changed since she'd been away. Nothing except the garden. She found her gaze pulled back to it. Just an hour of grafting here and there each week would have kept it maintained. Anyone could spare an hour here or there. But it wasn't the time commitment that had allowed the garden to run wild, Emily decided. It was the proving of a point. The garden was a symbol on public display that cried: *I have been neglected.* No. Worse than that: *I have been abandoned.*

"Well, I'm here now," Emily muttered.

It took her another two minutes to muster the will to leave the car. By then, she had seen her mother appear and disappear at the window more times than she could count.

The day was warm and heady. Above the village, the sky was cobalt blue with only a smattering of cloud. Emily sucked in a breath. The air tasted of fresh cut grass and summer flowers. The sun was warm on her skin.

Shutting her eyes for a second, she enjoyed the sensation. When she opened them again, she found her gaze drawn to the living room window, where her mother stood with her hands in the air. Sighing, Emily held up a finger and mouthed, "One minute."

She turned and looked down the empty street. It was as if she and her mother were the only two people on earth. It had felt that way growing up. The feeling remained.

Emily moved around to the back of the VW. It was an old model, the type where you had to pop the locks manually. The gearbox would need replacing soon, and the exhaust pipe was threatening to fall off, but Emily had fallen in love with it as soon as she'd sat behind the wheel. It was hers now, and hers alone. Just about the only thing that was.

She was about to unlock the boot and remove her bags, when she saw movement from the corner of her eye. A boy, thin and pale, and no older than seven or eight, stood on the pavement, staring up at her. He'd grown a little since she'd last seen him but he had also lost weight.

"Hello, Phillip. Nice to see you. Are you out here all alone? Where's that big brother of yours?"

Phillip stared up at her with wide, dark eyes. "Matthew's at home."

"No church today, then?"

The boy shook his head. "Have you come back?"

The knot of anxiety in Emily's stomach grew a little bigger.

"Yes, I have," she smiled. "In fact, I'm going to be teaching at your brother's school in September. Won't that be a nice surprise for him?"

Phillip shrugged. "What about when I go there?"

"I expect so." Phillip had at least another three years before he went to the secondary school over in Bishopstown. Emily wondered if she really would still be teaching there. Immediately, a flood of doubt engulfed her. She wondered if she had made the right decision by coming home. At least her mother would be happy. That was something. And when Lewis Hemmingway had found out Emily was returning, he'd called her up straight away and told her he was happy, too. And if Emily happened to have a free evening once she was all settled in, how would she feel about having dinner with him?

And there was her new post at Bishopstown Secondary School. She was going to be an English teacher, with classes of her very own budding, young students, whom she couldn't wait to introduce to all the classics, as well as her favourite contemporaries.

Phillip was still staring at her with big, dark eyes.

"Well, you'd better run along now before your mum starts wondering where you've got to," Emily told him.

The boy frowned. His shoulders hunched. "Don't want to go home."

"Oh? Why not?"

"Dad's home. He's in a bad mood."

Emily stared at him and chewed her lower lip. She ruffled his hair. "Well, then, how about you help me carry these bags to the door? There's half a melted Snickers with your name on it if you do."

Phillip grinned. "Okay."

Emily handed him her shoulder bag and he dutifully carried it in both hands along the garden path. He stopped halfway and looked back. Emily's mother was in the window again, an ominous silhouette with her hands stuck on her hips. Smiling, Emily grabbed a suitcase from the back of the car, found a smaller bag for Phillip, and stepped onto the garden path.

Phillip returned, his spindly legs moving awkwardly beneath him.

Emily handed him the smaller bag and flashed him a smile.

Perhaps she had made the right decision after all. The world would still be waiting for her when she was ready for it. Perhaps getting a few years of teaching under her belt was a good thing. It would certainly offer up a lot more opportunities when she did eventually decide to travel.

Phillip scurried ahead, the bag swinging from side to side. Emily followed behind, smiling at her mother who had moved from the window and now stood in the front doorway, peering nervously out.

Emily had come home. It wasn't the plan she had intended. But it wasn't the worst plan she had ever made.

"Hi Mum," she said, kissing her on the cheek.

Her mother nodded. "I'll put the kettle on. Get rid of the boy. The last thing I need is Angus Gerard banging on my door, complaining I've cast a spell on his son."

Phillip stood on the garden path, peering into the house. From her bag, Emily produced a half-eaten Snickers bar and handed it to him.

"Your reward, kind sir."

No, she thought, watching him scurry away with a smile spreading across his face. It wasn't the worst plan she had ever made. In fact, perhaps it was one of the better ones. What could possibly go wrong?

She watched Phillip disappear. Still smiling to herself, she stepped inside and closed the door.

EMILY SWANSON RETURNS IN:

LOST LIVES

Emily Swanson is in trouble. A terrible mistake has destroyed her life and left her suffering from anxiety attacks. Moving to London, she discovers the former tenant of her new home is missing. Deciding to investigate, she soon finds herself fighting for her sanity—and her life.

(Turn the page for a sneak peek.)

1

SHE WAS DROWNING, pulled under by a froth of limbs and bodies, swept along by currents of voices, music, and car engines. Dark shadows circled her like hungry sharks. Hands and elbows pushed and shoved. Exhaust fumes and food smells clogged her nostrils.

This was the old part of the city, where archaic buildings stood side by side, defences pitched against the onslaught of the modern. There were no smooth walls here, no towers made of steel and glass. This was all shadows and sculpture, buttresses and winding alleys.

The crowd surged and spat her out, leaving her at the mouth of a narrow street. She paused for a minute, counting to four as she inhaled through her nose, to seven as she held her breath, then to eight as she exhaled through her mouth.

The early November air chilling her bones, she moved along the street, checking the address she'd written on a piece of notepaper, until she stood in front of a tall apartment building. A plaque above the entrance read: The Holmeswood.

A woman in her early fifties and dressed head to toe in chocolate fur waited outside.

"Paulina Blanchard?"

The young woman's voice was a whisper above the street noise. She was pretty: mid-twenties, pale skin and green eyes, with shoulder-length blonde hair scooped into a winter hat.

"I'm Emily Swanson. I'm sorry to keep you waiting in the cold."

Paulina nodded, opened the folder she was holding, and took her time to slide a finger down the appointments list.

"Emily Swanson," she said, punctuating the name with a tap of her finger.

The young woman nodded. "I lost my way. London is very big, isn't it?"

Paulina's eyes fixed upon Emily, who smiled uncertainly.

"You should have been here at three. I have another viewing in fifteen minutes with a married couple, financial types. So, I'm afraid we'll have to make this quick."

The letting agent pulled open the grand door of the building. As they stepped inside, the outside world fell silent.

"As you can see this is the foyer." Paulina removed her hat to reveal a head of tight, salt and pepper curls. "Mail boxes are on your left. The lift is on your right."

The exterior architecture may have been Victorian, but the interior was distinctly Art Deco. Faded red and white tiles made a sprawling grid beneath Emily's feet, while two great pillars flanked her sides. A stained glass design of birds and flowers filled the space above the lift doors.

Emily's gaze climbed the sprawling staircase that sat in the centre of the foyer.

"It's beautiful," she said.

"The Holmeswood used to be a hotel back in the day," Paulina explained. "After the Second World War, half the city was rubble and no one came to stay. The owners filed for bankruptcy, someone else bought it for a song, knocked down a few walls and turned it into apartments. Is it just yourself or do you have a partner?"

"Just me."

"Any children?"

Emily's fingers glided over the grooves of the lift doors then slipped inside her coat pockets. The young woman shook her head. "How many apartments did you say?"

"Thirteen. Four on each floor, with the penthouse at the top. Here on the ground floor, beyond the stairs, there's an old laundry room. But it's been out of use for years."

"Thirteen?"

"The owner's a superstitious type. Which is why we have a Twelve-A, and then the penthouse, Twelve-B. You'll be looking at Twelve-A." Paulina tapped her wrist. "That's three minutes up already and we haven't even made it upstairs."

The lift was slow and moaned like a rheumatic old man as the two women rode in silence to the fourth storey.

"Here we are."

A long, gloomy corridor stretched out before them. Faded blue carpet covered the floor. At the far end, a window let in little daylight.

"The tenant will be at work now," Paulina said, marching ahead. She stopped outside of apartment Twelve-A and unlocked the door. "Won't you come in?"

A small chandelier of imitation crystals hung from the high ceiling of the hallway. A coat stand stood in the corner, its arms empty like winter branches. A few metres ahead, the hallway turned to the right.

"There are original floorboards in all rooms except the kitchen," Paulina announced, continuing her rehearsed sales speech. "On your left, you'll find ample storage cupboards. Doors up ahead lead to the living room, bedroom and bathroom. Access to the kitchen is via the living room. Shall we?"

She moved down the hallway with Emily trailing behind. As Paulina pushed open the living room door, her face flushed scarlet.

"I'm sorry, but there appears to be a spot of mess. I'd specifically reminded the tenant to keep the place tidy in mind of today's viewings. Clearly, he doesn't know the meaning of the word!"

Emily was still in the hallway, staring at the chandelier.

"It's no bother," she replied.

The living room was tall and wide, with two leather sofas on one side and a dining table and chairs on the other. A tower of open boxes, newspapers and packing tape currently occupied the space in between. Three arched windows, which stretched from ceiling to floor, overlooked the city.

"It's quite the view!" Paulina enthused, her gaze burning into the tenant's heap of belongings.

Emily moved to the centre window and pressed her face against the glass. Down below, streams of people bobbed around like microbes in a Petri dish. She studied them for a while, before turning her attention to the mountain of boxes.

"Why is the tenant moving out?"

Behind her, Paulina shifted her weight from one foot to the other.

"His wife left him, went back to Germany, I believe. I suppose there's no point in him staying on in a big place like this. You have a job, I presume?"

Emily stared at the curious array of belongings. The remnants of a life together did not make such a big pile after all.

"I'm relocating."

"Oh?" When Emily did not elaborate, the letting agent emitted a sharp huff. "As I mentioned, it's not the cheapest of places."

"I can afford it."

Paulina flipped through her file. "We'll need to run some checks – bank references, credit scoring, that sort of thing – but I'm sure you wouldn't be wasting my time. Speaking of which, we should see the rest of the apartment. The kitchen is right through here."

Emily watched the woman as she skirted around the tenant's belongings and disappeared through a pair of saloon doors. She watched them swing like pendulums, and then returned her gaze to the street outside.

Grunts and groans and a plethora of curses ricocheted off the foyer walls as men dressed in overalls heaved boxes and furniture toward the staircase. Some insisted on using the lift for heavier pieces of furniture, but there was barely enough room to fit in a few boxes and an upended coffee table. Emily worried about the old lift as it creaked and rattled its way up and down the building. And she didn't like the way some of the men kept giving her accusatory looks, as if she took pleasure in watching them lug furniture up a hundred steps. If Lewis had been here he would have laughed and reminded her that the men were getting paid.

"Watch it!"

From her position on the staircase, Emily saw two men sway back and forth with her tan Winchester sofa. The knot in her chest tightened as they knocked into one of the pillars. She hurried back upstairs, narrowly avoiding a collision with more men coming out of her apartment.

Winter sunlight illuminated trails of dusty footprints and crept over the broken boxes, newspapers and clutter that had been left behind by the former tenant.

In the kitchen, a pyramid of boxes sat on the floor. She looked at each one, reading the labels. One read 'BATHROOM' in large black letters. Another box had been crushed on one side.

It was a nice kitchen, Emily thought, as she admired its tiled floors, high ceilings, and ample storage space. Back at the cottage, her kitchen had been small and cluttered, with an old coal oven that was expensive to fuel and a pain to keep running. But she had loved it.

It was all gone now. The cottage. The village. Her old life. From today, the city was her home, and all its noise and chaos were her neighbours.

An unpleasant sensation chilled the back of Emily's neck. The bottom half of the double-hung window was open a few inches. She pushed down on the frame but it wouldn't budge. If Lewis had been here, he would have had something to say about that as well. And now that was two things Emily would have to speak to Paulina Blanchard about.

A large crash directed her attention to the living room. She peeked over the swing doors to see that the sofa had arrived. The men who had carried it were busy wiping beads of sweat from their red faces. Emily wondered if she should apologise. Perhaps make them some tea. But then they would slow down. And she wanted them gone.

Now, more men were coming, bringing armchairs and

her dining table. She felt their eyes upon her. Blaming her.

Just like everyone had blamed her before.

Darting into the kitchen, Emily pressed herself up against the wall, wanting nothing more than to be left alone.

An hour or so later, her wish was granted. A stillness descended upon the apartment. The only sound was the soft hiss of the radiators pumping heat into the rooms.

Outside, the sun sank behind the towers and turrets of the grand old buildings, casting their exteriors in dark tangerine. Emily pressed her face against the living room window. Sunday evening in this part of the city left the roads empty. Across the street, a promenade of shops was closed. Only a cosy looking Italian coffee shop remained open. Emily could just make out a couple sitting in the window.

Her stomach grumbled. Anxiety fluttered in her chest. Unwelcome thoughts crept into her mind. Emily shook them away and returned to the kitchen.

Soon, plates and cups sat in clean cupboards, and pots and pans hung from hooks on the wall. Outside, night had descended, moss green and bereft of stars.

Emily yawned. She had yet to unpack the bedroom. And even though her body yearned for rest, her mind crackled like fluorescence. *Make your bed and you make your home.* Her mother's words echoed in her mind as she made her way through the living room and along the hall.

The bedroom was the same length as the living room but half as wide, and at least twice the size of her old bedroom at the cottage. The removal men had shoved her bed up against one wall, opposite a row of built-in wardrobes. Emily turned to face their mirrored doors and stared at her reflection. She wondered what she would do with all this space. If Lewis had been here, she wouldn't have noticed the emptiness. But Lewis was gone.

She felt her heart race a little. Her breaths grew shallow. Scratching the back of her hand, she eyed the suitcases and boxes on the floor. She pulled open the wardrobe door. Then frowned.

Sitting in the shadows of the wardrobe was a bulky black refuse sack, its drawstrings tied in a loose knot.

Whatever the sack contained did not belong to her. She had packed up the cottage herself. She had sealed every box and crate without help.

Curious, Emily poked the sack with a finger. Pulling on the drawstrings, she peeled back the edges and peered inside. A grey knitted cardigan stared up at her. Underneath were more items of women's clothing, all carefully ironed and folded.

She took out a blue and white blouse and held it up. It was part of a uniform. A nurse's perhaps.

She supposed it was possible the sack had been mixed up with her own belongings by the removal company. Then she remembered what the letting agent, Paulina Blanchard, had said about the previous tenant.

How strange, Emily thought, as she pulled more items from the sack and laid them out like bodies on the floor. Had the man's wife been in such a rush to leave him that she'd left her clothes behind? Had their marriage been so unhappy?

Emily stood up. A strange feeling washed over her; a sudden dizziness that knocked her off balance.

Leaving the clothes, she stumbled back to the living room, where her bag lay on the dining table. Pulling out a bottle of pills, she tapped one onto a trembling palm, then swallowed it dry. Her heart was thumping now. Her chest growing tighter by the second.

Finding the sofa, she lay down and tucked up her knees. She waited for the feeling to pass. For the medication to reach her brain.

What had she done? She was here, alone in London. With no friends. No family. Where she was a stranger.

I could disappear, she thought, and no one would ever know.

She stared out at the city, feeling small and terrified, until chemicals made her eyelids grow heavy.

Sleep came, and with it, a dream in which she ran through fields of spoiled crops. Something moved behind her, coming up fast. Women's clothing lay strewn between the ploughed rows, all soiled and sodden and forgotten.

ACKNOWLEDGEMENTS

Huge thanks and debts of gratitude to: my editor Kate Ellis for your excellent work, and for pointing out the limitations of Newton's Third Law when it came to getting Becky Briar out of that bunker; Alasdair Gray, Victor Martinez, James Oliver, Nancy Oliver, Valentina Perez, and Jenn Thompson for your continued support; my family, for everything; and Mr Smith, who is everything.

Special thanks to my readers, and to my amazing launch team who are always so encouraging.

A thousand thank-yous!

Malcolm

Printed in Great Britain
by Amazon